About The Author

Fredy Ilaviya is a published author from Mumbai, India. His debut novel, Walked Away With My Soul has garnered excellent reviews from his readers and fans. It proudly stands on Amazon.com with a rating of 4.5 stars. What has made this book most appealing is its vocabulary, characterization, volume and a brilliant climax. Fredy now comes up with his second book which is quite different from his first one.

This book essentially contains younger characters who, after leaving their college and entering the practical world, experience the real nuances of the working of the law and order system of our country. How they play with it and salvage their friend would be a story worth the wait.

Having a strong penchant for writing, Fredy always believes in writing for the masses. What's more important here is, his content is never boring as per his readers, no matter whatever may be its volume. He has, and will always strive for the betterment of the womenfolk of our nation through his books.

Fredy is an expert in English language with an IELTS band score of 8 on 9 (British Council). Having read the works of Ravinder Singh, Tejeshwar Singh, Preeti Shenoy, Shikha Kaul, Akarsh Raker and Madhuri Banerjee among others, the one he admires the most is Chetan Bhagat for his exemplary literary works, Revolution 2020 being his favorite novel. Fredy wants to make an indelible mark in the world of fictional writing and be known throughout the world for his books.

The best way to contact Fredy is through his official fan page on Facebook. You can also write to him at authorfredy@ yahoo.com.

FREDY ILAVIYA

Invincible Publishers

First published in India in 2016 by Invincible Publishers

ISBN: 978-93-86148-18-6

Invincible Publishers
F-55, Sushant Lok II, Hong Kong Bazar Lane Sector 57,
Gurgaon-122003

Opposite Kasturba Ashram, Radaur Distt Yamuna Nagar,
Haryana- 135133

For the Indian Judiciary system

For those who don't believe in giving or taking dowry

For those who marry their daughters and don't trade them off

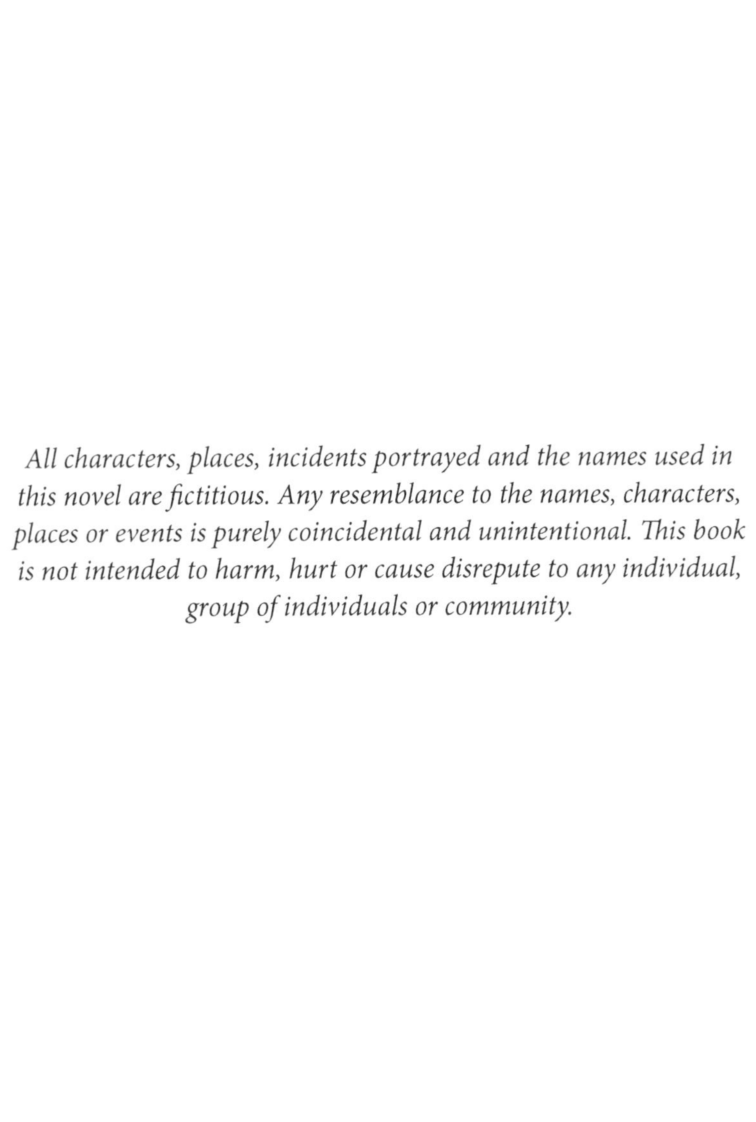

Prologue

Mumbai High Court
Dr. Kane Road, Fort, Mumbai.

Judge – Hon. Justice Sohrabjee Billimoria.

'... So, in Naina Daljeet Khurana rape case, vide chargesheet number 42313, taking into account the arguments submitted by Advocate Aakash Khanna, evidences against Daljeet Singh Khurana and Harjot Singh Khurana with reference to their confidential report by Blue Panther detective agency, statement of their servant Hariram and subsequent confession made by Harjot Singh Khurana, this court finds Daljeet Singh Khurana and his brother Harjot Singh Khurana guilty under sections 498A, 307, 376 and 34 of the Indian Penal Code and sentences them to a rigourous imprisonment for twenty years. It may be further noted that Naina Daljeet Khurana be granted a divorce immediately from Daljeet Singh Khurana without any further altercations and hearings for the same. This court is adjourned for the day.'

The moment Justice Sohrabjee Billimoria announced his verdict, all the attendees screamed in happiness and gave a standing ovation to him for nearly a minute. Everybody cheered and whistled as the joy in the hearts of Naina's parents knew no bounds. Naina wept incessantly as Nisha hugged her as tightly as she could. Soon, senior police constables hurriedly rushed to the witness box, handcuffed Daljeet and Harjot by their wrists and escorted them to judicial custody.

That evening...

'So we did it Kabir. Naina is all free now,' Aakash said.

'Yeah we did it man. We have won Aakash. Feels like today we have been just with our profession, though we chose a wrong way,' a defeated but overjoyed Advocate Kabir Dogra replied.

Aakash and Kabir, lawyers by profession, hailed from the same law college based in Mumbai. Having graduated around eight years back, they had started their own practice and were doing quite well in their profession. But something came along their way of practice that they had to bend the ethics, rules of the game and trustworthiness of one of their clients for the sake of justice. Only justice.

'Can you guess who's coming today to celebrate with us?' Aakash asked Kabir. They had come to Charmaigne Bar & Restaurant in Bandra to celebrate their victory in Naina Khurana divorce case.

'Not really… who?' Kabir asked with a puzzled expression.

'Karan. You remember him? Karan Verma… my classmate…,' Aakash helped Kabir place Karan, their college mate and now a practicing corporate lawyer.

'Oh! The one who delivered his baby in the canteen on his first day in college…?' Kabir recollected their good old ragging days in their college as they both burst out laughing.

'Yes… the same one! He's a practicing corporate lawyer and handles cases of big companies with relevant ease. I still remember, he always scored out and out in subjects of corporate law in every assessment,' Aakash said.

Meanwhile the waiter arrived with two menu cards and handed one each to Aakash and Kabir. They asked him to come after some time as Karan was to join them any moment.

'I simply don't understand some people,' Kabir said, 'I mean… how can they just ill-treat a human for the want of money? Those bastards tortured Naina to no avail… and reason? Money?! Is that why he took his marriage wows with her?'

Aakash went quiet on hearing this. He had nothing to say, or perhaps a lot to say on this. 'And here comes Karan,' he said, the moment he spotted Karan entering the arch – shaped wooden entrance of the bar.

After giving them a brief hug, Karan occupied his place. He

had just finished a long pending case with a well known corporate client of his, and badly needed a rendezvous with his best friend Aakash. 'So guys... finally done with Naina's case?' Karan initiated their conversation.

'Yes man... it was not less than a battle for us. But we decided to fight and were able to snatch victory from the jaws of defeat,' Kabir replied.

Aakash signaled the waiter to come and placed the order, 'A tower of Budweiser, one chicken tandoori and one plate paneer pakodas.'

'Guys I have been following Naina's case quite regularly. But I don't know the details; only those which came in the media. I want to know everything right from the beginning as this seems to be a very interesting case. My intuition says something else than what our media has to say,' Karan said.

'It came to me initially from Naina's family's side. Little did Naina know that the lawyer approached by them is none other than me,' Aakash replied as the waiter came with the items ordered. After carefully placing the tower of beer on the center of the table, he carefully divided eight pieces of chicken tandoori in our plates.

Then keeping the plate of paneer pakodas with mint chutney, he placed three empty glasses, pretty much broad, on our table and went. The practice was to fill the glasses from the tower by the patrons themselves. It was a perfect ambience for three lawyers to discuss their cases without anybody's vexation.

'I guess Aakash would be the best person to narrate this entire case to you Karan,' Kabir said as he filled everybody's glasses with the extra chilled beer from the tower to the brim.

Karan turned to look at Aakash with a tell-me-everything expression. Taking the first sip of beer from his glass, Aakash went on to tell everything about Naina's case to Karan right from the scratch. I would prefer to tell this story from Aakash's eyes as he rightly fits in the role of the narrator apart from being one of the protagonists.

So here we go!

Eight years ago…

1

J. L. Nathani College, Law Section
Churchgate, Mumbai

'Freak man, I'm really scared! These seniors... they'll make us do all sorts of crap in the name of ragging. Just keep looking down and quickly enter the class. If any senior spots us on the campus or corridor, we are bound to be stripped today,' Karan said to me in quick succession as we entered the main gate of J. L. Nathani Law College, one of the best colleges in Churchgate, a prominent area in south Mumbai.

'You are right man,' I said, 'but it's only a matter of a few days *yaar*. Give it a week or max ten days and these seniors will stop everything.' *Wow*, Karan thought!

Nathani Law College proudly spreads itself on a sprawling 5.5 acres of land which houses a 3-storeyed student community building having three auditoriums, two main buildings, a huge gymnasium right in the middle of the campus, a 3-storeyed library as well as parking space for two and four wheelers. There are two gates for entry and exit – the main one right opposite to the student community building and the other towards the left of the library. This college offers graduation courses in Science, Commerce, Arts and Law but specializes in offering the 5-year integrated BA LLB course for students aspiring to become lawyers. I and Karan completed our B. Com and took our admission in LLB in this college this year. We were mavericks as far as pursuing law as a career was concerned.

As we entered the corridor, we were suddenly spotted by a final year student who was probably summoned by his gang to keep an eye on any juniors to come. Soon the two of us were surrounded by five to six students of the final year, two of them being girls with boyish attitude. We were in a lather now – we couldn't even turn and go back!

'Hulllllo juniors! Your name? Address? Application

number? Come on come on come on… answer me quickly,' one of the senior students asked Karan who was already petrified by the very thoughts of ragging. 'K… K… Karan Verma. First year. I stay at Dadar. I mean… Dadar west. Application number 1411,' Karan answered in a frightened tone, much to the amusement of his seniors.

'And you?' a girl from the senior gang asked me.

'Aakash Khanna. First year. I live in Colaba. Application number 1462.'

'Hmmmm… First year… first day… a lot of things are waiting to happen with you both, eh?' Kabir, one of the boys from the senior gang said.

'L… Like?' an already scared Karan asked him.

'What? What did you just ask? You are our junior and asking questions to us?' a boy from the gang said to Karan and held him by his chin. We realized that it wasn't a time to ask questions but to comply with whatever the seniors asked us to do.

'Please leave him. This isn't the way… you are manhandling us,' I said to him.

'Oh…kay. Then let me *handle* you directly,' Kabir said and dragged me by my collars towards him. 'We are seniors and hold complete rights to rag cheeky little nuts like you,' he added.

'OK so what do you want us to do?' I asked the gang, especially to Kabir.

'Stare at her balls!' one of the senior gang members asked me, pointing out to a girl from their gang.

'What? Have you lost it?' Do you even know what you're saying?' I reacted in a firm tone.

This enraged Kabir who again held me by my collars and said, 'Now look babes… one more question you ask and we'll rag you in the worst possible manner. So stop asking useless questions and just comply with our orders. Do you understand?'

'What's going on there?' a voice from some distance held everybody's attention. It was Professor Desai, lecturer of labour laws and consumer laws for final year LLB. Needless to say, he knew each end every student from the senior gang who was trying to bully us.

'Nothing Sir, these are new boys here. Asking us directions for their class,' one of the students from the gang replied to him.

'OK. Go to auditorium no. 2. Professor Sinha is finalizing everything about your excursion visit and meeting with one of the bar council members. He wants to see all your classmates over there right now,' Professor Desai said.

'Release them. We'll see them later,' Kabir said to his gang and instantly released my collars.

'The score is yet to settle,' Kabir said to me and Karan as they started leaving for the auditorium.

***

Horrified by Kabir's last statement, I and Karan went to our class. It was a well-lit classroom with a seating capacity of around sixty students. Karan quickly noticed that most of our classmates were boys, in fact a majority of them. One could count the number of girls present merely on his fingertips! Both of us occupied the second bench on the first row. In fact, all the initial benches in all the rows were unoccupied – a ritual practiced in almost all the classes of all the colleges!

'Man… I don't know whether we'll reach home in a single piece today,' Karan said to me, 'You heard *na* what he said while going?'

'We'll see Karan. Don't panic. They are all bark and no bite. If things go out of control, we know whom to approach,' I comforted him.

'Hmm. Lets' see. Oh… Sir has come…' Karan said as he saw Professor Naik entering the class.

Professor Naik had a very unique personality. His hair was curlier than maggi noodles and height not more than five feet. His paunch often compelled the students to think that he needed no more food to eat for the rest of his life!

'Good morning Sir!' the whole class stood up and wished the professor in unison who walked up straight to the dais without even bothering to wish us back or look at us.

'Good morning students!' Professor Naik said as he kept

a thick reference book on the table, 'Nathani College welcomes you all. This is first year section – A and I am Professor Deepak Naik, your lecturer for first and second year. I shall be teaching you practices in civil and criminal laws, some chapters from contract law, an overview of the bar council of India and some topics of gram panchayat laws. Friends, it is very important for all of you to understand what law is, why it has been formed and how it safeguards the citizens and the nation as a whole. There are laws for every single thing in our country. Marriage, divorce, business partnerships, driving a vehicle to even consuming liquor – everything comes to us with strings of law attached to it. Business practices, taking care of one's family and even making your profiles on social media comes under the purview of law. In the forthcoming years you will be taught various underlying principles and practices concerned with the adherence of law. You are the lawyers of tomorrow, and I sincerely hope that you will safeguard the law till your last breath. We shall start with our routine lectures from eight in the morning tomorrow. Thank you very much!'

All the students gave a round of applause to the Professor for his short but effective welcome speech. I and Karan, however, were a little fearful about Kabir's last words to us.

***

'I am going to buy all my reference books online. You get a variety of them at discounted prices,' I said to Karan as we turned towards the college canteen to have a quick cup of tea. But little did we know that there was a huge surprise waiting for us.

'Oh fuck… Aakash… look… those seniors… they are sitting there,' a bewildered Karan said as he saw Kabir and his gang loitering in the canteen. Two of the gang members also spotted me and Karan, so it was no use for us to turn back now. 'Come come come,' a girl from that gang shouted as she saw us enter the canteen. 'Freak man!' I murmured as we stepped in.

'Come, sit with us,' a student from that gang asked me. I had no choice but to comply with it. 'So… how was your first day?'

Kabir asked Karan.

'Yeah it was good. Naik Sir attended us,' Karan replied.

'So tell me… how do we settle our score now? Kabir asked me.

'Why? Is it mandatory to settle scores with seniors in this college? We have come here to study, not to settle any scores. Let's go Karan,' I retaliated with full force which no junior can even dream to do before his seniors in a degree college, especially on his first day.

'Now that's it. I was waiting for this moment. Now just do as I say without uttering a single word. Look boss, we are seniors. You just can't get away like that. So if you don't want to tarnish your image in this college on the very first day, just comply with our demands,' Kabir said to me.

'Aakash, see *yaar*, it's our first day and we are juniors. So let's not dig ourselves deeper,' Karan whispered to me.

Helpless, I asked, 'Tell me, what do you want us to do?'

'I told you earlier Aakash, stare at her balls. For five seconds without blinking your eyes,' the same student asked me, pointing to one of their gang members who was all cool in her attitude even after listening to all this. College students are perhaps immune to all this by the time they reach their final year.

I had no alternative but to obey to the nonsense spat on me. I, though unwillingly, stared at the breasts of that girl but couldn't see them for more than three seconds. The moment I shifted my eyes from there, the girl stood up and hit me hard on my head and said, 'You pervert! He asked you to stare at my eyeballs, not these balls!' All the gang members laughed their hearts out on me while I was all in sweat by then. Karan wished he could get some magical powers which would enable him to disappear from there!

'OK now you… what's your name?' Kabir asked Karan. 'Karan… Ugh, Karan Verma,' he replied.

'Fine! So guys, what would you like Karan Verma to do?' Kabir asked his friends. They came up with weird options that pushed Karan into a black hole.

'Shave only on the left side of your face for ten days,' someone from Kabir's gang suggested.

'No! Distribute flavored condoms in Naik Sir's lecture tomorrow,' came another raunchy idea.

'OK, do one thing,' one of the girls from the gang suggested, 'Act as if you are delivering a baby. Right here, right now.'

Karan went into a state of shock. Helpless that he was, he stood up to perform. 'Ooh… aah… O God…' he tried to act. But this amused no one from the senior gang.

'What are you doing? Come on, do it properly,' Kabir said, rather commanded.

'OK, everybody lift him and put him on the table in the lying position. Only then he'll get that feeeel,' one of the girls from the gang said. Four guys from the gang quickly stood up and cleared the mess from their table which consisted of a couple of books, some pens, empty dishes of samosas and three bottles of Pepsi. Before Karan could protest, they lifted him and put him on the table in the lying position.

'No… please… I can't do all this… please spare me…' Karan pleaded to the gang, fully aware that he was only hitting his head against a wall.

'Oh come on man! Can't you even entertain your seniors this much? How are you going to stay till your final year in this college then?' Kabir asked him while I was a mute spectator to all this.

'Just act for a minute and set yourself free,' one of the boys from the gang said to Karan who was now cornered from all sides.

Now Karan did what he hadn't done all his life – he kept his bag below his head like a pillow and broadened his legs, much like a pregnant woman who'd deliver anytime. Not only Kabir's gang, but everybody present in the canteen paid a grim attention to him. Even I couldn't suppress a smirk.

'Come on Karan! Push… push… a little more…' all the guys from the senior gang started shouting as Karan started to act like a pregnant lady. He screamed on the top of his voice which amused the entire canteen. Everybody present over there joined the gang, 'Push Karan… it's almost done… there, we can see the head… push a little more...' Finally Karan delivered his baby and everyone cheered him. Before anybody could congratulate him for his delivery, he lifted his bag, got down from the table and ran away from the canteen with me as fast as he could!

That evening…

'So Aakash… how was your first day today?' my father asked me.

'Don't ask dad… I and Karan were in a pickle, but somehow managed to save ourselves. We were the royal victims of ragging today.'

'What happened son? Anything to worry?'

'Not as such, but we were made to do some of the most stupid things of this world,' I said, not wishing to disclose the details.

'Look Aakash, every newcomer in a degree college mostly faces all this, though it is now banned in many colleges and hostels in our state as per Maharashtra Prohibition of Ragging Act. Enjoy it while you do it, but if you feel that they start crossing the line, report it to the competent authorities. And don't hide anything from me,' dad said.

'But why they have to rag the newcomers dad? Can't they welcome us in a sober way?' I asked.

'Don't expect that Aakash. Seniors find a different type of fun in ragging their juniors. It's not that they have any hatred with them; consider it their way of welcoming their juniors and just let it go. But I again repeat – never let them cross their limits.'

'Sure dad.'

2

'Now consider a scenario wherein a person X willfully comes to assault someone, say Y, fully knowing that he might cause grievous injury to Y, or even death. Assault has already been established the moment X came near Y with or even without a lethal weapon.' It was Dr. Iyer's lecture in our class. Dr. Iyer was an expert with relevant sections of the Indian penal code or IPC. Everybody was listening to him with rapt attention as it was a very serious and important topic - assault. I and Karan wrote as fast as we could to make rough notes of whatever we could gather.

'Now if Y retaliates, leading to a skirmish between the two, it's often a who-remains-wins type of situation. Here, the psychology of the person who initiated the assault, X in this case, is either to kill his opponent or at least cause grievous injury to him. This is also referred to as grievous bodily harm. Now this leads to two scenarios - either X kills Y or injures him. If he kills him, he'd be arrested under section 302 of IPC, and if he injures him, section 307 would be applicable, which is referred to as attempt to murder. Now X's fate depends upon the evidence found, witnesses, if any, and the strength and defence of his lawyer in court,' Dr. Iyer concluded his topic for IPC sections 302 and 307.

'Any questions?'

'Sir what if X instantly kills Y and flees from the crime scene?' one student from third row asked the Professor.

'In that case, police will initiate their investigation and arrest all the suspects. They'll even look for evidence. Then it depends in which way their investigation goes.'

'Sir, suppose X kills Y but immediately surrenders himself before the police. Will police show any empathy to him?' Aarti asked.

'Of course not! A murder is a murder. X may have confessed to his crime but he is still a murderer. He will still be booked under section 302,' Dr. Iyer replied.

'But Sir, suppose if X tries to kill Y with a sharp weapon and in that scuffle, he is unintentionally killed by Y in self defence. Then will Y be held punishable by court?' Naina asked Dr. Iyer. Her unique question turned many a head towards her.

I instantly stopped making my notes the moment I looked at Naina. I just forgot the murder sections, Dr. Iyer, his lecture and even my own self. I carefully observed her pista coloured dress which was well matched with her oasis green dupatta. Her hair covered almost a third of her face which she tucked sideways every now and then. It may sound a little strange, but cupid's arrow struck me right there, even though a murder case was being discussed a few moments ago!

'In that case Y's fate will be decided on the strength of his case and his lawyer's arguments in court. But technically he being a murderer, he'll be kept in judicial custody till his case gets completed,' Dr. Iyer answered Naina's query.

***

I was all quiet in the canteen, sipping my usual cup of chai after our lectures with Karan. He sensed my silence at once and asked me, 'What happened man? All OK? You seem to be disturbed since Iyer Sir's lecture...'

'Karan, you saw that girl who asked Iyer Sir that question?' I asked.

'Which girl?'

'*Are* the one who asked Sir that if Y kills X by mistake then will he be punished...' I attempted to describe the one who stole my heart at first sight.

'Yeah I saw her, though I faintly remember her face now. Why what happened? You know her?' Karan asked.

'I wish I could...'

'What?!' Karan exclaimed. 'What's going on man?'

'N... Nothing Karan. Let's move,' I said and stood up.

'Hullo hullo hullo... Where to? We were to go to glory book stores to check out some second hand law manuals *na*'? Karan said and pulled my hand to let me sit back.

'You go *yaar*… I'll go tomorrow,' came out my reply.

'Anything about that girl?' Karan pulled his chair and sat again.

'I like her Karan. I really like her. It's as if I was waiting for her…' I said.

'What? Are you… I mean… You don't even know her name Aakash… Then how can you say that –' Karan snapped back as I interrupted him.

'Is it necessary to know someone's name before liking her?'

'No… I mean… Huff… I don't understand all this. Tell me properly Aakash, what's going on in your mind?'

'Karan,' I went on to convey my feelings, 'often it happens that we are in search of true love and a compassionate partner all our lives. Then to satiate that need we marry the one whom we don't even know. Most of us. But sometimes God sends our would-be soulmate right before us. Then it is upto us to know who he or she is. Today when I saw that girl for the first time, I realized at once that she's the one made for me. Now I don't really know how I have to proceed with this. But Karan, I have to proceed. I have to proceed.'

Karan was awestruck on hearing all this. He had no inkling that I had fallen for that girl so immensely, and more than anything else, was willing to take things forward with her.

'Look Aakash, we don't know her whereabouts. We don't even know where she stays and most importantly, whether she is single or not. So on what grounds do you – ' Karan said as I interrupted him again.

'Can I ask you for a small favour Karan?'

'Why are you even asking that?'

'Can you find out her name and other details by any means? More than anything else, I want to know whether she has a boyfriend or not,' I said.

'If you are that serious Aakash, just give me a few days. I'll dig all the stuff related to her. But while I do that, I want you to promise me one thing.'

'What?'

'Analyse your feelings carefully Aakash,' Karan said, 'If you feel that it's just a passing thought, leave it where it is. Proceed only if you are hundred percent sure. I don't want one-sided affairs and all that.'

'Done bro,' I assured him.

In the next few days Karan did whatever he could to extract all the necessary details about Naina. He befriended her best friends, Payal and Aarti, and swiftly asked them about Naina without being obvious. Once he even followed Naina discreetly when she was on her way back home. This way, he came to know her residence which was in SBI staff quarters in Mahim. In a matter of ten days flat, he gathered enough details about Naina and gave them to me, for I was desperately waiting for it.

***

'Contemporary Political Theory by J C Johari,' Naina said to the librarian. She had come to the library to borrow a reference book on political science. The librarian handed over the book to her after she signed on the register kept to maintain the records of the books borrowed. She chose a quiet corner in the library and started copying some notes from the reference book. But somehow she didn't find the relevant stuff in it as the language was too technical for her, she being a first year student. She went back to the librarian to return the book in exchange of another when I was taking a book from him.

'Take this back and give me Principles Of Social And Political Theory by Barker Earnest,' she said to the librarian.

'This book has just been taken by him,' the librarian said as Naina turned towards me when I was busy filling my details in the library register. The moment I gave it back to him and turned towards Naina, I was awestruck. I couldn't believe that the one I really liked was standing so close to me, looking at me!

'Hi!' I greeted, partly to introduce myself to her and partly to start a conversation.

'Hi!' she reciprocated. 'By when will you return this book to the library?' she asked me.

'This book?' I asked, looking at the fat reference book I had just borrowed.

'Yeah. I also need it to copy some notes.'

'Oh… OK do one thing, you use it first. Meanwhile I'll complete my remaining stuff of Sociology,' I replied, offering the book to her which I had just borrowed.

'No no… it's OK,' Naina denied my offer, 'You complete it first, I'll use it later.'

'I am sure you can use it first. I don't need it that urgently,' I prodded.

'OK. I'll return it in an hour. Thank you!' Naina said.

'Aakash,' I introduced myself as I handed over my book to her.

'Naina. Thanks again,' she replied as she took the book from me.

***

'But how come you guys met all of a sudden…?' Karan asked me. We were on our way to have some notes photocopied that evening.

'Library. She wanted the same book which I had borrowed. And – '

'– And you must have given it to her without using it yourself, right?' Karan teased me.

'Right, bro. At least we got introduced to each other today. Come on man… I need to befriend her'.

'Mmmm…. Sounds exciting… *acha* listen, are you preparing for Agarwal Sir's project?'

'I am almost done with it. But it is very boring *yaar*… giving speeches before final year students! I mean… who the hell are they to judge us?' I asked Karan in an irritated tone.

'Even I am not liking it bro, but what to do? And you know the best part? Students from our class have to deliver their speeches before final year division C!' Karan said.

'So?'

'It's the same class where Kabir and the rest of his gang study!' he announced.

'Holy cow! *Gaye kaam se*! I am horrified to think what they'll do if one of us commits even a slightest mistake,' I lamented.

'Let's see. No need to get upset. We can't be in a pickle every time. We'll prepare ourselves as nicely as we can,' Karan pacified me.

In the next few days I, Karan and the rest of our class took to Professor Agarwal's project diligently. Everyone was excited to deliver their speech before their seniors on the topics assigned to them. It was during this period that I came closer to Naina on the behest of preparation of the project, she being my classmate. Everything went well between the two of us and we were very close friends by the end of the preparation period, so much so that I started preparing for the project with Naina instead of Karan. But something went wrong on the day of the project.

***

'Karan Verma,' Professor Agarwal shouted as his predecessor ended his speech which threw some light on the legal documentation language used in India. Karan came on the dais, fully prepared with his topic, Indian Succession Act. As he was about to begin, Kabir and his gang tittered as they remembered how Karan had efficiently delivered his baby in the canteen on his first day!

'Shhh… Quiet, back benchers! Listen carefully to his speech,' Professor Agarwal shouted at Kabir's gang. I think he was habituated of titters and comments of the seniors.

Karan gave a superb performance on the dais. All the final year students were awestruck on hearing him. He put forth some facts which even some of our seniors weren't aware of. He was followed by me; I too managed to give my best, though not as good as him.

I was followed by six more classmates of mine after which Professor Agarwal shouted, 'Next, Naina Gill...' The whole class went a bit quiet on hearing her name. Naina walked up the dais with the confidence of a lioness. She had prepared for the laws related to transfer of property. I gave her a mild thumbs up as she saw me. She had worn a three-quarter sleeved plain white formal top which complimented a well fitting plain black trouser. The moment she started her speech, there was an unusual silence in the classroom. Everybody listened to her with grim attention. I could hardly even blink my eyes as I saw Naina in a simple yet beautiful avatar that day. Naina went on with her monologue on various laws and protocols involved in transfer of property and...................... Kabir went in a dizzy state as he just kept looking at her.

It was a love at first sight for him too.

He mentally admired her simplicity... her beauty... her knowledge... all secretly. Once again, cupid's arrow had struck someone in J L Nathani Law College by virtue of the same girl. Kabir had lost almost all his senses by the time Naina ended her speech. All the students gave her a long round of applause including Professor Agarwal. I was extremely happy for her.

Days went by and I and Kabir, unaware of each other's feelings for the same girl, kept going deeper in our plans to entice her. Karan assured to support me in every way he could, to bring the right situation for me to propose my feelings to her. I and Naina were very close by the end of our first term, albeit only as *good friends* as I was yet to propose her. Over there, Kabir had some unusual, out of the way plans to propose Naina who didn't even know him, he being her senior. A few days later, he shared this with some of his friends who promised to help him in every way to woo Naina.

'What? I mean... what's the hurry?' a mystified Karan asked me. We were seated on the cemented benches bang opposite the student community building after finishing our morning lectures, a daily ritual we followed right from our first day.

'I need to know what she thinks about me Karan. We are good friends but I don't want to remain only as a friend for her throughout my life. I need to find out that if I convey my feelings to her, how would she react?' I said.

'Hmmm.... Your point holds water *yaar*. But when and

how are you planning to propose her? Look Aakash, Naina is a very different girl. She may have befriended you and all that, but don't forget that till date she has always kept you at arm's length. A single mistake in your approach and you may lose her for ever. So be very street smart while you propose her. May I ask you something dude?'

'What?'

'Will you marry her after we finish our college… I mean… if she says yes?' Karan asked me. It might have been a difficult question for him but I had a straight and simple answer for it.

'Of course Karan! I will surely marry her if she accepts my proposal. Karan it's not that I want to be her boyfriend till we are in college just because we have a good camaraderie. Over these months I've come to know her nature, her likes and dislikes, what she wants from life and how happy she wants to see her parents. I shall support her in all walks of life. Not only her partner, I'd like to be her best friend. Bro… I love Naina from the bottom of my heart. Wish I could convey my feelings to her as easily as I do before you,' I unburdened myself.

'Oh…kay… That sounds quite convincing. Don't worry Aakash. Your feelings for Naina have fully persuaded me as I've been observing you all these months. It's just that I was a bit skeptical whether you were ready for any long term goals for her or not... Maybe you might not be in a position for a commitment as of now… I just… I mean… thought so…' Karan said, running his fingers through his hair.

'I am fully ready for a lifelong commitment Karan,' I said as we got up to leave, 'Now it all depends on how she reacts to my proposal,' I continued as we exited the college gate. But little did we realize that Kabir's friends had eavesdropped most of our conversation as they were on the bench just next to ours. They already knew that Kabir had fallen for Naina. Enraged, they went up to him and told him everything they'd heard between me and Karan about Naina.

This infuriated Kabir to no avail.

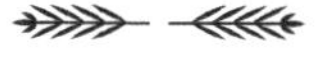

3

Kabir didn't attend a single lecture the next day. Rather, he couldn't. He came to the college and went straight to the canteen and texted his friend Krish who was in Professor Sinha's lecture.

Kabir: *Wer r u?*
Krish: *In sinha sir's lectur. Y u dint come?*
Kabir: *M in canteen. Cnt thnk of anythg... Need to talk to akash*
Krish: *K... hiz clas wil end by 11.15... v'l catch him in d campus*
Kabir: *K. Cum soon...*
Krish: *Yup. 20 min more*

Every passing moment was posing a million questions to Kabir – *How will Aakash react if I tell him to stay away from Naina...? What if he will tell about me to Naina...? What if Naina rejects my proposal...? What will my friends think about me then...?* When one in love, webs of stupidity often start to spin up. Usually, unnecessarily!

With the stroke of 11:15 AM, Professor Naik finished his lecture on cyber tort. I had absolutely no inkling that Kabir was waiting impatiently for me. As usual, I and Karan stepped out of the corridor when suddenly Kabir, Krish and a couple of his gang members appeared before us out of nowhere. Without paying any heed to them, we turned a bit sideways and continued walking when all of a sudden Kabir held me by my elbow with a force strong enough to disbalance my entire body. 'Wait Aakash, I need to talk to you,' he rebuked.

'What the hell Kabir...' I said as I vigorously shook my hand off his fist. I could easily comprehend that this wasn't a normal ragging stuff.

'Come outside gate no. 2. I am waiting there...' Kabir said and walked away with his friends. I just couldn't gather what happened in a matter of seconds! Was I daydreaming?

'What's the matter man? Why did he behave like that?' Karan asked me. I had no answer to it. 'Let's see. Come on,' I said as I proceeded with Karan to meet Kabir outside our college gate, exit no. 2.

***

'What's brewing between you both?' Kabir asked me, all worked up.

'You both? Whom are you referring to?' I asked in a puzzled tone. I still couldn't understand why he had called me outside the college campus which was a bit unusual.

'You don't know whom I am talking about? OK, let me clarify. Naina. I am asking about Naina. What's going on between you both? Are you involved with her?' Kabir asked in quick succession.

'Naina??? How does that matter to you? And who the hell are you to ask me with whom I am involved and all that?' I retorted with full force. *So that's the reason the moron asked me to come outside the college gate*, I thought.

'You bast... -' Kabir was about to cuss as Karan interfered, 'Mind your language boss. We are more proficient in bad words as compared to you.'

'You stay away from this, junior. If you utter even a single word in this, I swear you'll actually land up in a maternity ward,' Kabir said to Karan, reminding him of his sassy ragging days.

'Kabir, let's come directly to the point. There is no need to fight or argue. What's your point in calling me here?' I asked.

'It's quite simple, boy. Stay away from Naina. I like her and plan to propose her in a few days. Now if you come in between us, there'll be chaos. And I don't want any in my affair with her. Get that?' Kabir warned me.

'No! I don't get what you're saying Kabir. Firstly, you have no rights to call me like this outside the college campus and talk nonsense. Secondly, you again don't have any rights to tell me with whom I should keep a relation and with whom I shouldn't. And thirdly, if you believe in yourself and your feelings for Naina then go, propose her. Even I'll keep my feelings before her. Let's see whose proposal she accepts,' I replied to Kabir.

'What??? What do you think… is this some kind of a *swayamvar*, you moron?' Kabir shouted as a few students passing by caught our attention. In no time Krish shooed them away, they being our classmates – juniors!

'No, it's not. It's actually very simple; if we both love the same girl then we both hold equal rights to propose our feelings to her, isn't it? Rest depends on her,' I kept my point before an unsettled Kabir.

'Oh! So you are challenging me Aakash? OK, I accept it. You do your bit and I'll do mine. Neither of us tells her about either of us. One more thing Aakash… if she says yes to me, I bet I shall rag you again, this time right in front of her,' Kabir said, clenching his fists.

'Stop imagining and start making plans to propose her, senior! Wish you good luck' I said as we punched each other, fist to fist.

***

Professor Dr. Iyer announced the third project for the term for our class – Cyber crime: significance in social media platforms. The entire class of sixty students was divided in groups of ten each. As my luck would have it, Naina and I were in the same group, group – D. Thrilled, I called up Karan the same evening.

'Hi bro! How are you now?' I asked him. He had a viral since three days hence couldn't attend his lectures.

'I'm good Aakash. What's happening in college?' he asked.

'Iyer Sir has assigned a project on cyber crime for our class. And guess what… Naina and I are in the same group. You are in group – B,' I gave him the news.

'Oh! So when is the project to be submitted?'

'Next Wednesday.'

An instant idea struck Karan's mind. 'Dude, why don't you call Naina somewhere outside the college and propose her? I mean… I know… you are quite serious about her and proposing her is no joke. But don't you think it's the right time to put your feelings before her. See, you can always call her on the pretext of the project now, you two being in the same group. And boss… you better propose her before Kabir does.'

Karan's idea instantly filled up that empty portion of my brain which wasn't able to function as regards when, where and how to propose Naina. Calling her on the excuse of our project seemed to be a good idea, if not the best. I wanted to keep things simple and project myself the way I was.

'That's really a cool idea dude. But what do I tell her? I mean… we do share a good rapport, but my proposing her would be the last thing in her mind *yaar*,' I said, shifting the telephone receiver from my right ear to the left.

'Just be yourself and convey what you hold in your heart to her. I know, it'll be difficult for her to digest it initially, but she'll surely comprehend soon,' Karan said. His words moistened my parched mind.

'Okay. The sooner, the better. Let me meet her ASAP then,' I said and hung up.

'Hello aunty! Aakash here. How are you?' I called up Naina at her residence number. She had given her number to me a few months back and strictly advised me to call on it only if it was important.

'Hello *beta*. I'm good. You want to talk to Naina?' Naina's mother, Manju Gill, said. She didn't mind my calling their residence number as I had called up a couple of times earlier to speak to Naina for study related matters.

'Yes aunty…' I said, fumbling for words as I couldn't reveal to her that very soon I was going to propose her daughter.

'Just a minute…,' Naina's mother said as she kept the receiver on the table and went to Naina's room to call her. In a few moments, Naina came on line. 'Hi Aakash!'

'Ugh… Hi Naina! Hope I am not disturbing you?' I asked her the dumbest question ever.

'No no… tell *na*.'

'Actually Naina, our project needs a complete makeover. The topics which were assigned to Rohit aren't been completed yet and he says he'll take a few more days to do it as his father isn't keeping well these days. Why don't we catch up this evening somewhere and quickly redesign the entire project? Once it is planned, we'll quickly execute it and be ready by Wednesday,' I said whatever came in my mind. In all probabilities, I was confident that she wouldn't go to ask anything to Rohit as she hardly spoke with guys in college.

'Oh! OK then... We'll redesign it today itself. As it is, there are only four days left for the completion,' Naina said.

Yessss!!! My first step was done!

'So let's catch up at CCD of Dadar east at five sharp. Will it be OK?' I asked her.

'Yeah sure! See you then.'

***

Café Coffee Day, better known as CCD, proudly positioned itself at Dr. Ambedkar Road, Dadar east. It had circular glass tables kept in the center row with four wooden chairs per table. Cushioned cane chairs, slightly bigger in size, were positioned against the wall for two people. They were designed as if to serve only couples. Huge posters, black and white, depicting Hollywood celebrities adorned almost all the walls of the café. Waiters and stewards in crisp, dark purple uniforms were seen oscillating from the tables to the coffee counters. I reached at 4:50 PM and quickly chose a cozy corner having two cane chairs and a teapoy amidst them. To put it honestly, I was damn nervous. All these months I was just friends with Naina. But today I was to unbundle my emotions before her.

Naina arrived at 5:10 PM. 'Sorry Aakash… traffic… you know…'

'No! I don't know. I just came from Bihar this morning… how would I know about Mumbai's traffic?' I kept a straight face and joked as she burst out laughing.

'You didn't bring anything to write?' Naina asked me as she took her seat. I must admit she had dressed quite eloquently that day. Her orange coloured top matched with her orange *bindi* and camel brown ear rings, and complimented with her oasis green leggings. She never wore any heels as she never believed in going overboard, especially when it came to outer appearance.

'What will you have? First things first,' I said, passing a menu card to her which was kept on our teapoy.

'Hmmmmmmm.... I'll have a cold coffee with ice cream. You?' she said as she browsed through the menu. I just kept looking at her, secretly admiring her simple yet beautiful face.

'Hullo! What will you have?' she asked again, waving the menu card at me.

'A cappuccino,' I said as I waved at a waiter. He came to us, all smiles, took our order and went back, all smiles. *Hospitality at its core*, I thought.

'I hope aunty didn't get annoyed on my calling your residence number...' I started the conversation.

'Not at all. She's above all that,' Naina said, tucking her tresses sideways with her index finger. I just loved that.

'Actually Naina, I've called you for a different reason today,' I said, gathering all my energy from within.

'What happened? Is everything OK?' she asked in a somber tone.

'Yes, as such. Naina... actually I need to tell you, rather confess to you something that has been going on in my mind since many months. But before that, I want a promise from you,' I said.

'What promise Aakash? What are you saying? You are making me nervous now...' Naina said.

First love should be handled with great care, they say. Never let it remain as mere friendship. It hurts. But there are times when we just have to flip the coin and wait till it falls on the ground. I was about to flip my coin.

'Promise me that whatever I say today, you will take it in the right spirit. This is serious. It concerns my life. Whatever be your reply, we'll always remain friends.'

'Aakash... all well *na*? You sound different today... One moment, have we come here to redesign our project or is there something else?' Naina asked, completely unaware of the following moment.

'No Naina. Let me confess everything to you,' I said as I leant forward, 'Rohit is doing well in our project. Nothing has happened to his dad; he's fine. I'm sure our group will complete our project well before Wednesday. The reason why I have called you today is to confess my love to you. Yes Naina, I love you. I have loved you from the very moment I saw you in our class. Please don't take my feelings in a wrong way; I'm ready for a commitment. Just wanted to know what you feel for us,' I conveyed my feelings to the one I loved the most in the best possible manner I could.

Naina just kept looking right inside my eyes. I guess she wasn't upset or something. Neither she stormed out of the café nor did she portray herself as the most-surprised-girl as girls usually do. She was all quiet, just listening to me.

The steward came to us and placed a tall glass of cold coffee with a huge blob of chocolate ice cream on it, and a cup of hot cappuccino with a few white and brown sugar sachets kept on the saucer.

'Anything else Aakash?' Naina asked me in a low slung tone, shifting her cold coffee glass towards her.

'No. Nothing beyond this truth Naina. I know it is difficult for you to tell me anything in this right away. Take your time. I am in no hurry. But whatever be your reply to this, we will still remain friends OK,' I said in a chivalrous tone.

'May I give the reply to your proposal right away Aakash?' Naina asked me. My heart begin to race. I just couldn't react to her question. *What will she say? Will she allege me of abusing our friendship? Will she accept my proposal? Or will she just tell me to stay away from her?*

'Sure Naina…'

'Aakash it's not that easy for me to commit to any guy who proposes to me, however good and prosperous he may be. You're nice, you belong to a good family and we know each other quite well now,' Naina said, 'But may I come straight to the point? Love marriages are just not allowed in my family. We girls aren't allowed to enter into any relationship with guys. It might sound as an outdated stuff for you, but that's how it is. If ever my parents come to know that I have a boyfriend, they'll first kill me and later hang themselves by a ceiling fan. But they'll never accept all this, no matter what. So… sorry Aakash…'

Naina's words pierced a sharp arrow right in the middle of my heart. I kept looking at my cappuccino cup while listening to all this. I didn't even take a sip. Rather, I couldn't. I was expecting something similar, for love marriages are not so easily solemnized in our society, no matter how forward our nation goes.

'I do understand and respect that Naina. But if I were to ask you, what do you feel for me? What's there in your mind, keeping aside your family's views… what would be your reply then?' I again flipped my coin.

'I am not allowed to feel anything for any guy Aakash. My parents will search for a groom for me and marry me off to him. Nobody is going to ask my wish. So I do not have any feelings for you beyond your being my classmate and one of my close friends. That's it Aakash,' Naina said as she finished her cold coffee.

I faked a smile to comfort her. 'No issues Naina. At least I conveyed to you what I felt for you. And I thank you to react gracefully and not make a fuss of it. We both poured out whatever was there in our hearts. I feel so unburdened…' I said, coaxing my eyes not to leak. For months together I had been madly in love with this girl and waiting for the right time to propose her, but in a matter of moments she vaporized everything in thin air.

'May we leave? Guess there's nothing to talk on this now…' Naina said as she stood up. I was in no mood to go home. The serene atmosphere of the café forced me to spend some more time over there. 'I'll stay here. Need to spend some time with my own self. But Naina… we will always remain friends, remember *na*?' I asked.

'Yes I do… see you tomorrow,' Naina said and left the café. And me too. I just kept gazing at my cup. The cappuccino had turned cold by now.

So that's what is still followed in many customs in India even today. Girls aren't allowed to be in a relationship with guys of their choice. They are married off to the one decided by their family and extended family members. Here, she's never asked her choice. And such girls are educated even upto the Masters level! Strange, but true. And Naina Gill was a living example of such girls. Probably that's why she didn't harshly react to my sudden proposal. She even promised to be friends with me. I didn't touch my coffee; she finished hers. Minuscule thing, but worth a thought.

***

Days went by and everything was back to normal. I had accepted the fact that it was impossible for Naina to be in a relationship with anybody… that she was simply not a love marriage material. Karan did his bit in removing me from the fantasy I was living in since the day I saw Naina for the first time. Our project went superb with Professor Dr. Iyer making a special mention of it during one of the alumni meets in our college for the students of the 90s. On the other end, Kabir's whims for Naina had touched crazier heights. He would often bunk his lectures just to have a glimpse of her when our last lecture would finish. It's not that he was infatuated or something; probably he too liked Naina to the same extent as I did. But now that I knew Naina's views, I could actually foresee how she would react to Kabir's proposal. In any case, I had lost the one who stole my heart at first sight.

'What??? I mean… since when Kabir?' a perplexed Aarti asked Kabir. Kabir was her senior in school and hence they knew each other very well. Kabir had a plan in his mind to take her help in approaching Naina, for Aarti was our classmate and one of the closest friends of Naina.

'Don't ask *yaar*… just the day I saw Naina and since then she's hovering in my mind. Aarti, don't think that I'm lovesick or something. I really like her man… I'm even ready for a commitment,' Kabir put forth.

'Yeah but… I mean… I don't know how it will work. Because I know Naina. She is a very different type of girl Kabir. She does not even like any guy from our college. In fact, apart from studies she doesn't even talk about anything. I really wonder how she'll react to your sudden proposal…' Aarti said.

'Proposals are always sudden Aarti. Maybe they are planned, but for the one being proposed they are always unexpected, isn't it? I have a plan and need your help in it Aarti. Now please don't say no.'

'What do you want me to do in this? Should I convey your message to her or something...?' Aarti asked, still in two minds whether to comply with Kabir's request or not.

'Oh no, nothing of that sort. I shall myself propose to her. Look, just call her anywhere and I shall accidentally run into you both. Then give any excuse and leave from there. I'll milk the opportunity and convey whatever I have to, to her. Game?'

'What? But where will I call her Kabir?' Aarti asked.

'Hmmmm...' Kabir thought for a while and came up with a random suggestion, 'Phoenix mall, Lower Parel? I guess that'll be the best place.'

'Oh... kay. I'm sure you know what you're doing Kabir. For the sake of friendship I'll comply with what you're saying. Hope it won't spoil my friendship with Naina...' Aarti said.

'Not at all. Trust me Aarti, all will go well. Naina can never refuse me,' Kabir pacified Aarti, unaware of Naina's reply to his proposal.

'OK then, this Saturday I and Naina will be there in Phoenix mall by six thirty in the evening. Hope all goes well...' Aarti said as she crossed her fingers.

'I bet.'

Kabir started preparing himself for his grand proposal. He bought himself an expensive shirt from Van Heusen and corduroy trousers from Westside. He made everything look perfect in order to woo Naina in the very first attempt. Aarti didn't hint anything to Naina about her conversation with Kabir, as planned. She didn't even know that I had already proposed to Naina.

Aarti: *Hi baby... phoenix mall... 2day eve? Wat say???*

Aarti texted to Naina after coming home. It was Saturday, Kabir's D-day. Aarti did not hint anything about their visiting the mall as she wanted to ask Naina at the end moment. Everything had to seem impromptu.

Naina: *Phoenix mall??? Y suddenly....?*

Aarti: *Just lik dat babez.... Feelng bored :-(*

Naina: *:-) Okiez. Evn I wntd to hang out... mall seemz 2 b d* *best plac. Payal iz cmg?*

Aarti: *Nopes. Jst d 2 of us ;-) she has her projct submision on mon...*

Naina: *K... Wer do I meet u?*

Aarti: *Hmmmmmm......... lowr parel stn... 5:30 sharp?*

Naina: *Done.*

Aarti immediately called Kabir and conveyed to him the timings. He had fortified his plan to accurately bump into her and Naina. He instructed Aarti to first roam around in the mall with Naina and then go to the food court where he would coincidentally meet them. Then on the pretext of a phone call, Aarti would get up and swiftly vanish from there whilst being on her (fake) call. And that would be the time when he'd propose to Naina. Aarti agreed to his plan as everything seemed quite foolproof. But little did Kabir know that he was hitting his dart on the wrong board.

***

'Hey, let's have a look at the tee section,' Aarti said. She and Naina had reached the mall at 5:45 PM and were busy doing their window shopping as per Kabir's plan.

'Not again Aarti! This will be your fifth tee in this month,' Naina scolded and dragged her forward.

'Noooooo......' Aarti yelled but by then they had already passed The Chimps Tees Shoppe. She was extremely fond of tee shirts and would rarely repeat a tee, once worn in college.

Kabir was to bump into them at 6:30 PM sharp in the food court. Hence Aarti maintained their pace so as to reach the food court only by 6:20 PM. She wanted everything to seem original, though every moment was being faked by her.

After roaming the entire mall and whizzing past various showrooms of clothes, beauty care products, baby products, eye gear, health care products and the like, they decided to go to the food court to savour some of the finest burgers from Burger King.

'Two chicken tandoor grill burgers and two Pepsi,' Aarti placed their order to the steward as she reached for her purse. They were at the counter of the eatery which servers some of the choicest burgers.

The moment she removed a 500-rupee note out of it, Naina snatched it with her left hand and paid the steward with her right one. 'Keep it back, you bitch,' she said to Aarti.

'Naina... this is not fair *ha*... why didn't you allow me to pay?' Aarti playfully scolded, a registered trademark of girls when they get pleasantly annoyed.

'Quiet! Go, search for a table for us while I collect the stuff from here,' Naina said.

Aarti gazed all around only to see all tables occupied by either couples, families, groups or individuals, given that it was a Saturday evening. She could, however, spot a small table with two chairs from a distance and went on to grab it before anyone else could! Soon, Naina arrived with a tray in her hands containing two freshly made burgers and two tall glasses of Pepsi with mostly ice cubes in it. Aarti saw the time in her watch – it showed 6:30 PM. Her heart began to pace at a faster rate. But she didn't make it obvious and started to enjoy her burger with Naina.

Five minutes later she felt someone tapping her shoulder. She moved around to see – it was Kabir. 'Heyyy Kabir... how come here?' she asked him, trying to sound as normal as possible.

'Hi girls! One of my friends owns a watch showroom over here... had come to just catch up with him,' Kabir said.

'OK. Pull a chair *na*,' Aarti said as Naina gave her a stern gaze, signaling her not to welcome him. Aarti just winked at her.

Kabir helped himself with a chair and joined the girls. 'You'll have something?' Aarti asked him.

'Nopes! I just had my breakfast,' Kabir grinned.

There was an eerie silence for the next five minutes as nobody spoke anything. Swiftly, Kabir removed his cell phone from his pocket and discreetly dialed Aarti's number without making it look obvious, especially to Naina. Aarti's phone rang the very next moment, but before Naina could see its screen, Aarti quickly picked it up from the table and answered it, rather faked it, 'Yes mom?' Everything was going as per their plan.

Aarti slowly got up with her phone in one hand and her burger in the other. She faked Kabir's call and went a little ahead without making it obvious. 'So how do you feel law? Have you developed a taste for it? I mean… will you enjoy being a lawyer by profession in future?' Kabir attempted to initiate a conversation with Naina who was already nervous by now.

'Law is good. I don't know whether I'll take it up as a profession, but as of now it is very interesting,' Naina answered.

'Okay. Actually the purpose of my visit is different,' Kabir gathered all his strength and came directly to the point.

'You wanted to buy some stuff?' Naina asked.

'No, nothing as such. I need to tell you something Naina,' Kabir said. Naina was shocked to the bone on learning that Kabir knew her name, though being her senior. She started looking for Aarti all around the food court but simply couldn't spot her as she had already left the mall by then.

'Please don't feel uncomfortable Naina. I'm not a stalker,' Kabir said as he smiled. Naina just curved her lips a bit in response.

'What is it Kabir?' she asked him.

Clearing his throat, Kabir went on to open his heart, 'Naina, I know you from the day you gave a presentation in my class. Yes, you had given it in my section. You stole my heart the moment I saw you Naina.' Before Kabir could say anything further, Naina banged her glass of Pepsi on the table and got up. Kabir instantly stopped her, 'Wait Naina, please let me speak.'

'Now I understand why Aarti made a mall plan all of a sudden. And that phone call? No matter who calls her, she'll never leave me and go like that… So it was your plan, right?' Naina asked him. He had no answers to her obvious questions. He just kept telling her to wait and listen to him.

'Go on…' Naina said after much coaxing. She never wanted to create any scene in the crowded food court of the overcrowded mall.

'Naina, ever since I saw you, I've been madly in love with you. The way you look… the way you dress… the way you carry yourself… I mean… it's all so simple yet so beautiful! I have spent four years in this college but never proposed any girl. You are the first one I've approached. And trust me Naina, my feelings for you aren't a passing thought. I'm quite staid about what I'm saying and even ready for a commitment. If only you –' Kabir said as he was interrupted by Naina.

'One moment Kabir. Before you go any further, let me tell you a few things about me. I don't want to take this discussion further. One, I'm not allowed to keep any relationship with any guy by my family. Two, love marriages are not allowed in my family. Three, no matter how studious or wealthy one may be, my family will never accept him because they haven't chosen him. So Kabir, let's stop this here itself. No hard feelings.'

Kabir was awestruck by Naina's sudden disapproval. He couldn't utter a single word further. He was expecting something positive, he being one of the few handsome guys of my college. But Naina gave a repeat performance to him too, after me.

Before Kabir could react to Naina's age-old traditional stuff, she picked her handbag and left the food court. Kabir simply couldn't digest that his much awaited evening would end up on a bad, pretty bad note.

4

'Never even imagined that Naina would react to my proposal in this way man!' Kabir said to Krish. They were in the queue, waiting for their turn to come. The process of registration for their final year exams had already begun, with exams being just two weeks away.

'Shit happens *yaar*. Just forget it. We have to fully concentrate in our exams now. Leave her; she has many more years to study but we'll pass out this year,' Krish pacified Kabir.

'You're right,' Kabir said as he pulled a face.

In no time the final year LLB examinations commenced. Kabir, Krish and the rest of their friends started to diligently prep up for the same and spent most of their time in library. Kabir gave his best in every paper and was damn confident about his results. We never spoke to each other since the day we met outside the campus; a strong feeling of hatred had crept in our minds. He disliked me to the core of his heart, and so did I. Perhaps, we both might have felt that either of us was responsible for Naina's refusal to us. He never ragged or made fun of either me or of even any of my classmates. He was, perhaps, a changed person ever since he proposed to Naina and got rejected. I could relate to him easily, for I was given a similar reply by Naina. We could have chosen to be friends then, but probably our egos and the brewing resentment for each other stopped us from doing so.

Soon after the declaration of the final year results, Kabir, who managed to score 61% aggregate, left the college after a happening send-off party which lasted all night long at Krish's place. Every member of his gang passed out; no ATKTs, no repeats. With this we entered our second year with more responsibilities and work load, especially on the practical front. Remembering the sections of IPC along with a million more things related to law ate up a major portion of twenty four hours we had in a day. As time flew by, we engrossed ourselves deeper in our studies and understanding the law and order machinery of our country which could, and still can be personified with a slow moving bullock cart on an express way.

After two years…

'Karan, has the time table come?' I asked Karan. We were heading towards the office of Advocate Madan Mathur, one of the close friends of my father.

'Yes. They've uploaded it on the college website. I'll bring a printout for you tomorrow,' Karan said. We were at our best in preparing for our final year examination.

'Freak! When's the first paper?' I asked.

'23rd April.'

We reached Advocate Mathur's office in ten minutes. My father had categorically instructed me to visit him before my exams to take some last minute tips from him.

Advocate Mathur's office was situated on the first floor of Gulistan building on Sir P. M. Road, Fort. As we entered, we were greeted by his receptionist who asked us to take a seat. No sooner did she inform him about our arrival than we were called in his chamber. Maybe because it was lunch time that we didn't have to wait to meet him.

'Come in… come in *beta*,' Advocate Mathur welcomed us we entered his chamber. I must admit, he had a posh office.

'Good afternoon uncle! How are you? Dad advised me to have a word with you before my exams, so…' I said as we sat on the plush leather high-back seats kept opposite to his table.

'Yes yes… he told me last evening over the phone. So *beta*… what'll you have? Tea, coffee, juice…?'

'Coffee would suit us uncle. Thanks! By the way he is Karan Verma, my friend. He also studies in my class,' I introduced Karan to Advocate Mathur as he stood up and shook hands with him.

'Good! Please sit Karan,' Advocate Mathur said as he picked up the receiver of his phone and dialed the pantry, 'Three coffees.'

'So when are your exams starting from?' he asked me.

'23rd of next month uncle. We have prepared very nicely for all subjects but still need some guidance from you on the do's and don'ts while preparing for the exams,' I replied.

Over the next thirty minutes, Advocate Mathur briefed us on correct ways of preparing for our papers. He advised us some techniques on how to memorize IPC sections with relative ease. He also touched some basics on how to do the analysis of case studies which were compulsory questions. Being one of the close aides of the joint secretary of Bar Council of India, he also gave us some important tips on the functioning of the same.

'Thank you so much uncle! This is surely gonna help us a lot,' I wholeheartedly thanked him as we stood up to leave. Being a busy lawyer who would charge his clients on an hourly basis, he managed to give us enough time by virtue of his friendship with my father.

***

My exams went pretty well. Everyone of us – I, Karan, Naina, Aarti and Payal – scored above 65% aggregate. On the day of our result, we five decided to have a party at Karan's uncle's sea facing bungalow at Juhu which was lying vacant as he resided in Canada. I and Karan ordered a crate of Kingfisher Pint beer along with pizzas from Dominos. It was, perhaps, our last night together as from the next day everyone of us would scatter in different directions in an attempt to give a meaning to the most complicated thing of this world – life!

'So Karan… what next for you?' Payal asked Karan. We were seated in a circular pattern surrounding a short, round table on which we kept our beer cans and pizzas. Naina was highly adamant on not having beer initially, but couldn't last before Aarti's coaxing for merely half a pint. Things had gradually mended between the two of them after Kabir's mall incident. Naina took time, but she forgave Aarti. I and Naina, well, forced ourselves to forget what had happened between us. Surprisingly, till date, only Karan knew amongst us that I had proposed her once.

'I have decided to work under a reputed lawyer or a

solicitor for at least two years before I start my own practice. It's useless to start on your own without a practical exposure,' Karan said, downing the remaining beer in his can in one draught.

'Hmm… that's true,' Aarti said, 'I am also going to work as a junior counsel under a lawyer named Advocate A. H. Khan. My dad has recommended him as they were college friends.'

'Now we'll come to know what it takes to actually safeguard law and justice. There'll be no Iyer Sir or Desai Sir to guide us when we'll be handling our cases,' Payal quoted the obvious, moving her finger on the rim of her beer can. Her statement forced everyone to think in which way to proceed further.

Biting a slice of my pizza, I intervened, 'There's no need to think so much. We all are lawyers now and theoretically well versed with the law machinery. Now we just need to plunge into the system and do our work with utmost diligence. As for me, I am going to open my own office and operate from Worli. Dad has assured to help me in my initial set up. I shall learn things, though slower than Karan, but all by myself.'

'Wooooooow!!!!!' Payal and Aarti roared in unison, almost shaking the walls of the decade-old bungalow. I stole a glance at Naina; she didn't react much to what I said. First love never dies… its remains sometimes haunt you to no effect. But we had moved on. Rather, we had to.

'Naina, what are your plans?' Karan asked her.

'Definitely I won't work as my parents won't allow. Don't know exactly…' Naina replied.

Everybody went silent on hearing this. We all knew the situation at Naina's house… that she won't be allowed to work after college. But that's the way she was brought up. She couldn't, in the wildest of her dreams, even imagine to rebel against her parents. Maybe she was paying the price for being born as a girl child in a conservative family.

'Oh… whatever…' Aarti said and put her arm around Naina's shoulder to lighten the moment. 'At least you will not have to slog like us *na*!' she humored. Naina gave a coy smile to her.

We five kept reminiscing our college days and future plans till nine at night. Had it been an only-guys gang, we would have sat till the wee hours of morning. But we restricted ourselves till 9:00 PM as strictly suggested by the girls well in advance.

'Karan... Aakash... keep in touch OK. Wherever we'll be, we'll always be in touch,' Payal said as the girls stood up to leave. They had already hired a cab which arrived at nine sharp right opposite our bungalow.

'Sure Payal! I'll make a Whatsapp group of all of us tomorrow itself!' Karan said as he hi-fied her. *At least, this way I'll stay connected to Naina*, I thought. In no time the girls left for the cab which was waiting outside the gate. Was it the last time I saw Naina?

After six months...

'*Are* but what's the hurry *yaar*?... I mean.... We're just twenty four!' Payal wondered. Naina had called her and Aarti to Navratna Restaurant, one of the finest vegetarian restaurants in Mahim, to break the news.

'You know *na* Payal... nobody asks me in these matters. Dad is already in talks with them; their close relative happens to be his colleague,' Naina said. Her father, Siddharth Gill, served as assistant branch manager in State Bank of India, Mahim west branch, and was five years away from his retirement. He strictly followed the only-gents-to-decide-everything code in his household. Even Naina's mother was not allowed to voice her opinions freely in certain matters. It's not that Mr. Gill bossed around; rather he gave full freedom to Naina and her sister Nisha to study as much as they wanted. But in matters of marriage and relationships, he never allowed anybody's interference.

'But Naina... we've just come out of college barely six months back. We aren't a marriage material yet. We need to move around, see the world and meet people before we come to terms to marry a guy who we won't even know!' Aarti sermoned.

'There's no place for such ideals in my house Aarti,' Naina said as she wiped her moist eyes with her bare hands, 'We girls have to pay the price for being born as girls to the last penny in certain matters.' Aarti and Payal empathized with Naina, but there was nothing in this matter that they could do for her.

'So is the guy fixed?' Aarti asked after a brief silence of ten seconds.

'Yes. His name is Daljeet Singh Khurana. They stay as a joint family in Santa Cruz west. He's up to starting his own business soon,' Naina announced.

Payal and Aarti weren't happy at all on hearing all this whereas it should have been the other way round. They knew Naina's nature since years; all what they feared was Naina's raw age for marriage in a joint Punjabi family.

'I hope you are doing the right thing Naina,' Payal said, keeping her palm on Naina's hand.

'The best part is, I am not doing anything here; I am only doing what I am told to do,' Naina replied.

'Told to do or forced to do Naina?' Aarti interfered, 'Hope you are not forced into this marriage…'

'Whatever Aarti, but the fact remains that I have to comply with what my parents tell me. That's the only way out for me,' Naina said, staring at a faraway tower from the glass walls of the restaurant.

'*Chalo* let's take all this on a positive note. He may be a good guy, we never know. God plays his own games to send our partner in our lives the way he wants. Let's hope for the best,' Payal said, shooing the air of seriousness away.

At Naina's place…

'No no… they aren't asking for much,' Naina's father said to her mother. The duo were discussing about Naina's marriage on the breakfast table.

'Still… what are their demands?' Naina's mother asked him as Naina joined them for her breakfast, unaware about the topic of discussion going on. 'Good morning mummy, good morning dad,' she greeted them for the day.

'Good morning *beta*,' they reciprocated in unison, 'Come, sit.'

'Nothing much,' Naina's father continued, 'only eight lakhs cash, fifteen *tolas* of gold and a Maruti Swift DZire car.'

'What? This much? How are we going to arrange so much

Siddharth?' Naina's mother wondered.

'Dad... are you talking about my dowry?' Naina intervened, much to the annoyance of her father.

'Naina, you may have studied law which tells us not to give or take dowry. But practically it doesn't happen that way *beta*,' her father replied to her. 'We have to follow certain give-and-take practices to survive in this society,' he continued.

'That I agree dad. But just look at their demands! Cash... car... gold... I mean... are you wedding me or trading me off to them?' Naina said, realizing the very next moment that she went slightly overboard in putting her point.

'Naina! Don't interfere in matters that you don't understand, first thing. If I don't give anything to your prospective in-laws, I bet you'll never be able to marry anyone,' her father replied spontaneously.

'That'll be fine. Even I don't want to marry anybody who takes away your entire retirement fund. What will you and mummy do after you retire if you give away all your savings like that?' Naina exploded. She couldn't stand the nonsense put forth by her would-be in-laws to her parents.

'Shut up Naina! Don't talk nonsense. You want people to say that we couldn't even get our daughters married off in a nice way?' her father said. Before things could take an acrid taste, Naina's mother told her to go inside. 'This is not done... simply not!' Naina murmured as she scurried to her room.

'Don't worry Manju, I shall take a loan on my provident fund. One of my LIC policies which I had taken in 1995 will also mature in four months' time. If need be, we'll even sell off our plot of Nashik,' Naina's father said. 'Today's children... God help them! Now who'll make them understand that there are certain codes of conduct to live in our society. And if give and take is there, it is there. We can't change that,' he continued as he got up.

'But Siddharth, we need to think about Nisha's marriage as well,' Naina's mother said.

'That we'll see. Let it come. But I don't want to let such a prospect slip out of our hands for Naina. They are a well knit Punjabi family Manju. And Daljeet plans to open his own car service center very soon. Our Naina will be a queen there; can't you foresee how happy she'll be in that house? *Are* what's the value of the stuff demanded by them before our child's happiness?' Naina's father expressed his mental bliss, fully unaware of what his daughter would have to face in future.

***

In no time Naina's marriage ceremony preparations kicked off with a boom. Her father kept on complying with every demand of the Khuranas, big and small. In an attempt to keep them happy and their demands fulfilled, he mortgaged his provident fund and even sold off his plot of land at a much cheaper rate, all in a matter of fifteen days flat. Naina was a mute spectator to all this as she wasn't allowed to speak in these matters.

'Now at the last moment they are saying that they want the ceremony to be at Club Emeralds Hall,' Naina's father said to her mother. They were on their routine discussion of give and take post dinner in their bedroom.

'Club Emeralds?! That'll overshoot our budget. There is no end to their demands Siddharth…' she said.

'What to do? Club Emeralds people charge on per plate basis which includes everything – hall rent, flower arrangements, music by the most reputed and happening DJ, photo and videography and car arrangement to take the bride. They charge Rs. 800 a plate, veg, non veg and *thali*,' he said. Hope he would have understood that marriages do not come with an insurance cover!

'Good lord! That'll be like… more than three lakhs!' Naina's mother wondered. Women are expert with mathematics, but only in certain situations.

'Yes, I've already calculated that. But we have to do it Manju. For the sake of our daughter.'

In the last few days before the marriage ceremony, the preparations went on at a much faster pace. Invitation cards were delivered, purchase of jewelry for Naina and ethnic dresses for everyone was completed well on time. A special makeup and hair stylist for Naina and Nisha was hired for the entire day of marriage.

Naina's parents had invited everyone of us for the D-day. Karan, Aarti and Payal graced the occasion right from nine in the morning till the time she was bid farewell by her parents. Naina's parents had left no stone unturned in making all the arrangements and fulfilling all their demands to the best of their ability and budget. For my own reasons, I didn't attend her marriage, for I simply wouldn't be able to see her take marriage vows with someone else. She was my first love and still so. I couldn't palate the fact that she belonged to someone else now. Karan coaxed me a lot to come and gracefully bid her adieu on her wedding day but I couldn't do so. I spent the entire day in a bar with her invitation card in one hand and a glass of whisky in the other. Naina's marriage extinguished the flame which was burning within me since years. Finally I could, albeit half-heartedly, convince myself that she was Mrs. Daljeet Khurana now, not Miss Naina Gill.

Naina's married life took a violent turn later on, with me to play a pivotal role to salvage her from it.

After four years…

5

Naina's in-laws stayed as a joint family right from the beginning. Her husband Daljeet Singh had a brother, Harjot Singh and a sister, Amanjeet Kaur. Harjot Singh was married to Lovleen Kaur and they had an eight year old son named Arvinder who was a spoilt brat. Daljeet's father, Tanvir Singh Khurana was a living example of a sexist and largely advocated the gents-first theory. Daljeet's mother, Gurpreet Kaur was a kind lady but rarely acknowledged by anyone in their household.

Naina was disliked by everyone from the very day she stepped in that house. She was made to do all the household work which included cooking, doing the dishes, watering the plants in their garden and even moping the floor at times. They didn't give her the respect and position in their house which she rightly deserved, though they had received quite a stuff as dowry from her parents. Naina was reduced to merely a servant in that house. Lovleen would make her do all the work whilst being a couch potato herself and enjoying the daily soaps all day long. In an attempt of give his daughter a good life, Naina's father had given away a major chunk of his savings to her in-laws in the name of generally-practiced-give-and-take. But everything turned topsy-turvy for Naina. Still she hadn't complained about her situation to her parents, only Payal and Aarti knew about her. They coaxed her on numerous occasions to either rebel against her in-laws or go back to her parents. But Naina knew her parents' mind-set and the amount of money that was blown up to get her married.

A typical day in Naina's life…

'Yuck… Naina! What the hell is this?' Lovleen screamed as she took the first sip of her morning tea served to her by Naina.

'What happened *didi*?'Naina lowered the flame of the gas and rushed to Lovleen in the drawing room.

'Couldn't you add *saunf*? I have always told you to add it in my tea, don't you know that?' Lovleen said.

'*Saunf* is finished *didi*. I'll bring it today. Sorry…' a meek Naina replied.

'*Saunf* is finished so you added ginger in my tea, you dunce?' Lovleen asked.

'I thought –' Naina was about to reply as Lovleen interrupted her, 'Please, no need to think anything in this house. Just do as you are told. Let the thinking part be done by us.'

'OK *didi*, sorry again,' Naina said and went in the kitchen and continued to prepare breakfast for everyone.

'Naina, I asked you to iron my clothes last night, didn't I?' Daljeet stormed inside the kitchen and asked Naina.

'This iron doesn't heat up enough *jee*. We need to give it for repairs. Why don't you ask Arvinder to get them ironed from the laundry?' Naina suggested.

Slap!

'Can't you go by yourself? Do you have a bone in your leg?' Daljeet said as he hit her on her ear. 'Finish everything and get it repaired. You are the most irresponsible person we've ever seen. Now what will I wear?' a pathetic Daljeet asked.

'OK,' Naina replied with teary eyes. But her tears were habituated of not spilling out over a period of time. She had adjusted with these demons and continued to work like a slave all day long without giving a damn to her own identity.

After preparing *chola bhaturas* and tea for everyone, she packed three sandwiches for Arvinder's school tiffin. She kept herself too busy in her household work to think about the wrongdoings of her in-laws. Whenever her parents or sister called her up, she would portray herself to be a happily married woman and speak as if she was living on a magic carpet. She had made friends with her circumstances. Being a daughter of middle-class parents, she never even dreamt of opposing anyone in that house. Daljeet's mother was a mute spectator to all this as she wasn't paid heed to by the devils and the witch who resided in that house.

'I am dead tired. Need some relaxation Naina. Remove your clothes,' Daljeet said as he pulled Naina towards him, it being his mundane ritual every night. Naina had no choice but to fulfill her duties as his wife. Even her sex life was blown out of proportion as Daljeet would have sex like an untamed dog almost every night.

'Daljeet, why don't we have a child?' Naina asked him, loosening the lace of her night gown.

'We aren't using any protection. Now if you are unable to give me a child, what's my fault in it?' Daljeet said as he helped her remove her gown.

'But Daljeet, we are married since almost four years now. It's high time we need to think about this. Why don't we visit a doctor and see where the problem lies?' Naina expressed her concern. Maybe at this juncture of her life, a kid would have kept her in solace.

Slap!

'Don't suggest me on things I already know. It's you who has to give birth, not me. So if you are unable to do it, why should I get myself humiliated before the doctor?' Daljeet slapped, came on her top and did the act.

'When will your dad give me the amount we've been asking? Can't he foresee that we'll swim in money once my car service showroom starts? Taking a franchise of 3N Car Care is a big deal. How many times I've to beg before him?' Daljeet said as he dressed up. He couldn't stay on top of any woman for more than five minutes, I guess.

'Never! I've told you people several times not to ask for any money from him. He has given you enough Daljeet, being a service-class person. Now don't expect anything from him,' Naina replied.

'You bitch… how can you and your parents be so selfish? Can't you see how much money I'll earn once my showroom starts? You middle-class people… you'll never understand what is dreaming big.'

'Arrange for the money yourself Daljeet. Don't pressurize my father for it. Use the money he had given to you during our marriage. But don't demand anything from him now,' Naina said as she put her clothes on and went to sleep.

Daljeet and Harjot were hellbent in taking a franchise of

3N Car Care, a reputed car service showroom. They were told to have a three thousand square feet shop and deposit five lakhs as a collateral. All the money received in marriage was already spent but they wanted to desperately start their business. And Naina's father seemed to be an ultimate solution towards funding the same.

Few days later…

'She is not in favour of approaching her father Harjot,' Daljeet said to Harjot. They were in their regular drinking session at Amrut Bar & Restaurant, one of the shoddy bars in their neighborhood.

'It's been years that you've been asking her to talk to her father. Can't she understand that we'll start minting money once our showroom starts?' Harjot said in despair.

'Bloody slut! I have done the biggest mistake of my life by marrying her. She bears our surname but still supports her parents. *Are* come on man… a person working on a managerial level in a government bank… imagine what money he must be making every month! Can't he give us just twelve lakhs?' Daljeet ideated.

'If he wishes, he can. But he just doesn't want to see us prosper in life. And your Naina… even she carries the same genes. I don't know what will happen if this opportunity also goes out of our hands!' Harjot wondered.

That night, their drinking session continued longer than usual. They kept on ordering pegs after pegs of Royal Jumerine, a cheap whisky which could abruptly alleviate their devilish senses while suiting their pockets. Their senseless conversation about pressurizing Naina to arrange for twelve lakhs from her father went on and on with no concrete conclusion. Daljeet had been asking Naina for the same since more than three years. But Naina had seen the amount of money which was spent by her parents to get her married, hence she was firm in not involving her father's money in any matters of the Khuranas.

'Brother, let's teach her a lesson tonight. Let's do something that'll force her to bring money from her father tomorrow itself.

Who the hell is she? A goddess or something? Here we are having a budget whisky like Royal Jumerine instead of Black Dog and there she is happily living by her own terms! Get up Daljeet,' Harjot said, barely able to stand on his feet after seven pegs of whisky.

Daljeet didn't react to Harjot's sudden *alcoholic arousal.* He was as high as Harjot, having had the same whisky. After an eerie silence of ten seconds, he too stood up and said, 'Let's go to that bitch. Tonight shall be a hell for her. Let me see how she doesn't bring money from her father.' The duo paid the bill and barely managed to exit the bar.

That night. 01:37 AM…

'Get… get up N… Naina. W… we need to talk… talk,' Daljeet managed to speak as he vigorously shook Naina by her shoulders who was fast asleep. She was habituated of Daljeet's post-drink-late-night-arrivals but never dared to ask him the reason.

'What happened *jee*?' Naina asked him, still half asleep. She couldn't even open her eyes properly.

'Y… you fucking bitch! You've left me in the m… middle of nowhere and asking me wha… what happened *jee*?' an inebriated Daljeet replied.

'*Are* at least tell me what happened?' Naina said, realizing the very next moment that Harjot was standing behind Daljeet. They had entered Naina's room and locked the door from inside.

'*Bhaiya*! What's happening *jee*?' Naina asked Daljeet as she quickly covered her shoulders with a bedsheet as she was in a sleeveless night gown.

'Shut up! N… Now listen to me c… carefully Naina. Convince your father to g… give us twelve lakhs in a w… week's time or else we'll s… spoil you tonight,' Daljeet said to Naina, violating all the marriage vows he had taken with her before four years in a split second by uttering those words.

Naina was too petrified to say anything or react to this. She kept looking at Daljeet with an unexpressive face.

'What? C… come on, get up. Get up and call your d… dad right now. Tell him to arr… arrange for money as soon as po… possible,' Daljeet reprimanded as he dragged her out of bed.

Something instantly clicked inside Naina. 'I don't want to talk about this Daljeet,' she said and hurried to leave the room. Daljeet held her by her arms from her back and pounced her on the bed before she could realize that something of that sort could happen.

'Daljeet! What are you doing? Enough is enough! Leave me…' Naina raised her voice as Daljeet slapped her thrice. 'You whore! C… calling me by my name…?' Before Naina could defend herself, Daljeet held her by her legs and asked Harjot to hold both her hands. Harjot followed suit.

'*Bhaiya*! Please… don't do that… I tie rakhee to you… I call you *bhaiya*… please don't do that…' Naina wailed, only to fall on deaf ears.

Suddenly someone knocked the door of that room. 'Harjot, I'll manage h... her. You go and see wh… who's there. Manage and come back. Quick!' Daljeet said to Harjot. Harjot went to the door and asked, 'Who's this?'

'*Sahab*, I am Hariram. Is *didi* OK?' Naina's screams hit upon their servant Hariram's ears who was fast asleep in the kitchen adjoining Naina's bedroom.

Harjot opened the door to the minimum extent. 'Yes H… hariram, wh… what do you want?' he asked.

'*Sahab*, I heard Naina *didi*'s screams. Is she OK?' Hariram asked. Little did he know that Naina's mouth was sealed by Daljeet's palm.

'Yeah she's OK. J… just a bit of stomach pain. We are att… attending her. You go, s… sleep,' Harjot replied in an intoxicated state. As he was about to close the door, a suspicious Hariram asked again, 'Does *didi* need anything *sahab*?'

'No! G… go now,' Harjot replied and closed the door immediately. 'Daljeet… wh… what now?' he asked Daljeet.

'Tell us… w… will you bring m… money from your father or n…not?' Daljeet asked Naina who was moaning in pain.

'No! I won't Daljeet. I won't. I never knew you'd stoop so low for the want of money… Why don't you earn yourself instead of begging before us?' Naina replied as she attempted to loosen Daljeet's hand which was gripped around her neck.

'Are you s… sure of this?' Daljeet asked as he loosened his

grip.

'Have I ever given in to your demands all these years?' Naina replied as she managed to sit, 'And you… Harjot… I never expected that you'd crouch down too. Now I understand… you all are the same. But I am not going to victimise myself. I am leaving this house right now. Forever.'

Before Naina could leave the room, Daljeet and Harjot drained all their diffidence and even humanity and did what can send shivers down anyone's spine. They lifted her and again pounced her back on the bed. Before she could scream for help, Harjot stuffed a cloth in her mouth, then took out a condom from his pocket and gave it to Daljeet. Daljeet went on her top, unzipped his trousers, lifted her gown and did the inevitable – he raped his own wife right in front of his brother. In the fury of his unaddressed monetary demands by Naina, he penetrated her vigorously like a wild bull. Harjot too could no longer resist his hunger on seeing all this. Naina couldn't utter a scream as her mouth was tightly stuffed by Harjot. As usual, Daljeet finished his act in five minutes.

'Come Harjot, rape the bitch,' an infuriated Daljeet said as he got up and zipped his trousers. Harjot was all set to rape the one who had been tying him *rakhee* ever since she had married his brother.

Harjot too used a protection and repeated the same act on Naina with thrice the force. Probably there was no need of a cloth to stuff Naina's mouth then as she was too shocked to react to the situation. She just stared at the ceiling fan and tolerated everything. Two hefty men… forced penetrations one after the other… Naina's life had taken a violent turn in a matter of fifteen minutes flat.

'Huff… she's too good br… brother…' Harjot said as he got up and buttoned his jeans.

'That's the only w… way to teach a l… lesson to people like her,' Daljeet said. As he was about to leave, he saw the most dreadful thing which he hadn't seen all his life: Naina was bleeding profusely from her privates. A good portion of her bedsheet was soaked in her blood. Forcible penetrations of two demons had taken its effect. She was unconscious by now and lay on the bed like a lifeless body.

'Oh my God! Harjot... look...' Daljeet said as he saw Naina lying unconscious on the bedsheet drenched in her blood.

'Oh fuck! What do we do now?' Harjot panicked. Few pegs of Royal Jumerine had topsy-turvied the life of an innocent girl.

'We need to take her to the hospital immediately Daljeet, no time to think. If something happens to her, we will come in a serious problem. That's why we used a condom... at least our semen traces won't be found in her so it won't be medically proven that we have raped her,' Harjot added.

In no time Daljeet stuffed the blood-stained bedsheet in a huge plastic bag, took the car keys, lifted Naina and took her to glory hospital along with Harjot. They merely admitted her in the hospital, filed the admission form and told the doctor on-duty that all of a sudden she started bleeding and fell unconscious. But the doctor was wise enough to understand the truth. He strictly advised Daljeet to remain in the hospital, he being her husband. In no time Naina was shifted to ICU and gynecologist Dr (Mrs) Sulbha Sareen was called to attend her immediately.

After thoroughly checking Naina in the ICU, Dr Sulbha came out. 'I'd like to talk to her husband. Looks like a rape, though there are no semen traces found,' she said to Dr Chavan, the on-duty doctor. Dr Chavan immediately summoned one of the ward boys and asked him to call Daljeet from the waiting lobby downstairs. But neither Daljeet nor Harjot was present in the lobby. They had left Naina all alone in the hospital to fight her battle. When Dr Sulbha was informed about this by the ward boy, her doubt was clear.

'Call the police,' she said to Dr Chavan who immediately informed the local police. Head constable Tawde and constable Gaikwad arrived in twenty minutes. But seeing Naina's condition, they asked Dr Chavan to call them once she regained her senses.

Next day...

Naina regained her consciousness at around 8:30 AM. 'Call Sulbha madam, quick,' Dr Chavan said to the on-duty nurse as soon as he saw Naina open her eyes slowly.

'Sulbha madam has gone home Sir. She told that she'll be there by nine in the hospital,' the on-duty nurse said.

'OK. Meanwhile call anyone from the police station. Tawde *saheb*'s duty must have been over by now,' Dr Chavan said.

By nine, Dr Sulbha as well as constable Darekar were present in the hospital. 'Looks like a rape case. But no semen traces are found inside her vagina. Multiple forced penetrations have been made. I guess she is in her menses and hence couldn't tolerate forced sex. Her husband and his brother admitted her last night at around two forty five and left her all alone over here. We've been trying to contact them but I guess they have filled in wrong address and contact number in the admission form. Now only she can give all the answers,' Dr Sulbha detailed everything to constable Darekar.

'Any signs of attempted murder?' the constable asked.

'I guess so. Her neck had red marks when she was admitted. Looks like her neck was gripped by someone before raping her.'

'OK. Can we meet her madam?' constable Darekar asked.

'Yeah sure. Even we'll need to ask her a few questions before furthering her treatment,' Dr Sulbha said as they proceeded to Naina.

Naina lay like a lifeless body on the bed of the ICU. She just kept staring at the walls. Probably the tragic memories of the previous night were haunting in her mind.

'Good morning Naina! How are you feeling now?' Dr Sulbha asked her. A drop of tear spilled from Naina's eye as she heard the tender voice of Dr Sulbha.

'Please call Aarti and Payal. I need them,' Naina uttered her first words in the hospital.

'Who are they?' Dr Sulbha asked her, as mildly as possible.

'They are my friends. My best friends,' Naina said and started crying miserably. Dr Sulbha tried to console her; it took her a few minutes to convince Naina that she was totally in safe hands.

'Naina *jee*, look, we need to take your statement. Be flexible and tell us everything that has happened with you. Only then we'll be able to help you out,' constable Darekar said.

'Keeping her palm on Naina's hand which had a saline drip attached to it, Dr Sulbha said, 'Naina, tell everything to police. You were brought in a very bad state over here last night. The two men who admitted you went away within minutes. They have written incorrect contact details in the admission form. We can't trace them. We'll be able to contact them through you only. Are you in a position to talk?'

Naina nodded, indicating an affirmative reply. 'But first call my friends… Payal and Aarti,' she said. Constable Darekar took their numbers from Naina and called Payal and Aarti to the hospital. Aarti first called up Payal to ensure that it wasn't a prank call. But when Payal told her that even she had received a call from the constable, they were assured and rushed to the hospital in twenty minutes.

Naina wept and wept as she saw her friends… her pillars of strength. They hugged her tightly and gently asked her the reason for her sudden arrival in the hospital. In the next thirty minutes Naina recounted the entire incident of the previous night, leaving everyone present near her infuriated to no level. Constable Darekar recorded the minutest details in his notepad and left.

'I need to talk to Aarti and Payal privately,' Naina said to Dr Sulbha.

'Yes, you may. But don't talk much as you still need a lot of rest. I'll keep coming. Take care Naina,' Dr Sulbha said as she left the ICU ward. In an hour, Naina was shifted to a private ward as she was out of danger.

'What the fuck is all this Naina?' Aarti asked her.

'It's the sum total of my sufferings of all these years.'

'I have told you several times not to tolerate their bulllshit Naina, didn't I? What if something grave would have happened to you?' Payal intervened.

'That's the life of every middle-class girl Payal. Do we have a choice?' Naina replied.

'Of course we have, who told you that we don't have one? Now you will only do as we say,' Payal reprimanded.

'What?'

'Let's inform your parents and call them here, first thing.

Secondly, you are not going back to that bastard Daljeet's house. If he tries to come in your life by any means now, I shall kick him so hard on his groin that his testicles will pop out of his mouth,' an exasperated Payal announced.

'Shhh... Payal... talk slowly,' Aarti said.

'Whatever. I'm calling Manju aunty,' Payal said and took out her phone from her purse.

'Hello, Manju aunty...? Good morning aunty, Payal here.' She called up Naina's residence number.

'Yes *beta*, good morning. How are you?' Naina's mother answered.

'I'm fine. Aunty... please come to glory hospital with uncle as soon as you can,' Payal said.

'Glory hospital? Why? Everything OK Payal?'

'No aunty. Nothing is OK. Please come here as soon as possible,' Payal said.

'*Are beta* but...' Naina's mother was about to say something but just heard a beep in response.

***

The moment Naina's parents and sister arrived at her room, they were stunned like hell. They didn't have a slightest hint that their daughter was in hospital all night long. Naina's mother hugged her as the mother-daughter duo wept incessantly. Payal and Aarti kept a straight face; they didn't console Naina's mother as they gave her some time to digest the situation.

'*Didi*... what happened? Since when are you admitted here?' Nisha, her sister, asked her.

'Last night,' Naina replied.

'But what happened? And where is *jiju*?' Nisha asked.

'Don't take that bastard's name,' Payal intruded. Fury had taken over her by now.

'What? What are you saying Payal...?' Nisha asked. Payal just turned away.

'Naina *beta*, what is all this? Tell us the truth. You people are hiding something from us I guess. Aarti *beta*... what has happened?' Naina's father asked.

'They both raped me last night, dad,' Naina collected all her strength and replied to her father. It's unimaginable for a middle-class girl to admit to her own father that she's been raped. But Naina did it.

'What?' Naina's mother asked and instantly got up.

'Yes mummy. Last night Daljeet and Harjot raped me.'

'Daljeet *raped* you? What are you talking Naina? You made all this fuss because your own husband *raped* you? What's going on?' Naina's father asked.

'One second,' Aarti intervened as all heads turned towards her, 'Sorry for what I am going to say now uncle. You always wanted Naina to get married to some suitable boy in a good family and all that. That's OK till there. But do people like you ever care to see what life their daughters lead once they are married off, or in my own words, traded off? Do you even know what kind of a beast that Daljeet is? Probably you don't, uncle. He and his brother Harjot have been pestering Naina to convince you to give them twelve lakhs as they want to start their own car servicing showroom. When Naina repeatedly turned down their request, they did what a well bred person can never even think of doing. They both stormed in Naina's room last night, strangled her neck almost to the point of suffocation and raped her like untamed beasts. I don't know about you and aunty, but I and Payal will surely stand by Naina and see to it that Daljeet and his family is punished.'

There was a grim silence in the room. Naina's father kept looking at Aarti with teary eyes which would spill any moment. Naina was, perhaps, waiting for a response from him.

'Naina, my baby, I am so sorry for whatever has happened. Let's go home. I am not sending you to Daljeet now,' Naina's mother said in a chocked tone. She didn't invite further questions and answers.

'*Are* but where is *jiju*?' Nisha asked again.

'Nisha, please don't call him by that name. He and his brother left your sister all alone over here last night and ran away like mice. They are disgusting to such an extent that they filled in wrong address and contact number in the admission form. So please…' Payal said.

Nisha went quiet. Probably she didn't have anything to say then. She was tougher than her sister in these matters and mentally resolved to be by her side.

'Thank God! The police didn't come…' Naina's father said.

'Police has already recorded Naina's statement, uncle,' Aarti said, 'But I am pretty sure that Daljeet's family will grease their palms and walk away with this.'

'Huh! Wait and watch,' Payal said.

A few days later Naina was discharged from the hospital. Neither Daljeet nor anyone from his family called up or cared to come to the hospital. The local police arrested him and Harjot on the charges of raping Naina, but sensing no legal moment from Naina's family's side, the Khurana brothers heavily bribed the inspector in charge of their case and walked free.

***

'Look baby, we aren't your enemies. We know your nature right from our college days. But there are times in life when we have to take a final stand,' Payal said to Naina. She and Aarti were at Naina's place. Ever since Naina was discharged from the hospital, they were regular visitors to Naina's place to comfort her. All they were waiting for was the right moment to ask Naina to rebel for what she had lost.

'What stand Payal? What stand? My own husband rips me apart for what? Merely twelve lakhs? Dad spent a fortune on my marriage, agreed to all their demands, big and paltry. Still their hunger kept on increasing. What could I have done…?' Naina replied as she stared outside her window.

'Well, you could have done a lot in that too, but forget it. Tell us, now what do you intend to do?' Aarti asked.

Naina just shook her head with an I-don't-know expression.

'Naina, do you respect your parents' upbringing? Do you respect your education? Most of all, do you respect your own self?'

Payal asked in one go.

'Yes Payal, I do,' Naina said.

'Then let's teach that dog and his family a lesson of their life. Let's drag them to the court,' Payal suggested.

Naina didn't say anything. She didn't refuse either. Aarti added, 'Look Naina, nobody can play with us the way they want. Uncle gave them more than what was required to marry you, but you saw *na* what happened? Do you have any idea how disgusted that family is? And you still call that devil your husband?'

'I want my life back, Aarti, Payal. I want my good old days back,' Naina announced.

'Good. Now you'll only do as we say Naina. No red tape, no questions. Firstly, let's send a legal notice to Daljeet,' Payal said. The mere thought of sending her in-laws a lawyer's notice pushed Naina in a black hole with zero gravity. But Aarti and Payal assured her that they'd be by her side at every step of her legal battle, and that she needn't worry.

Payal and Aarti logged in to the lawyers' forum of India from Nisha's laptop. They found the contact details of a lawyer, Advocate A. Khanna from Dr Annie Besant Road, Worli. They booked his appointment online for the same evening and informed Naina to be ready by 6:00 PM.

'Must be a good lawyer *na*? Look at his achievements!' Aarti wondered as she scanned through the notice board which had newspaper cuttings of the lawyer's success stories. Naina, Payal and Aarti were waiting for their turn to meet Advocate Khanna in his office outside his chamber.

'He indeed is. I'll woo him if he's handsome too; I'm telling in advance,' Payal chuckled.

'Naina Khurana,' the receptionist called out as two men came out of the lawyer's cabin.

Aarti, Payal and Naina got up to proceed for the lawyer's cabin. The moment they entered, they received the biggest shock of their life. Advocate A. Khanna was no one but me – Advocate Aakash Khanna, B. Com, L.L.B.

6

It took a while for me to digest what I just saw. 'Aarti... Naina... Payal! Heyyyy.... Hey girls! How are you? How come here today?' I asked them.

Naina wasn't able to face the situation; I could easily guess it from her body language. Payal and Aarti were pleasantly surprised to see me in my black and white attire working in my own office. 'Aakash! So Advocate A. Khanna is nobody but you?! Wowww!!! Good!' Payal said.

'Please sit, girls, don't be formal. It's your own office,' I said.

'It's been like... what? Three or four years...?' I said, trying to recollect when we four had met the last time.

'Yes. Four years, at least. How is your practice going on?' Aarti asked me.

'Good. Pretty good actually. Ever since we completed our LLB, I started practicing on my own. Initial two years were quite tough as I was new to the procedures and common practices. But now I am set... almost,' I replied as I called for my office boy. I observed that Naina hadn't uttered a word till then.

'Four coffees and two packets of Good Day biscuits, quick,' I said to my office boy. He followed suit.

'Payal, Aarti, nobody likes to visit people who wear either white coats or the black ones. I mean, doctors or lawyers. What makes you guys visit a lawyer's office today? All OK?' I asked.

'No Aakash, nothing is OK. We have come to take your help. Naina is in deep trouble,' Payal said.

Payal's words came to me like a sharp blow of a fist right on my nose. *Naina had turned down my proposal years ago only to get married as per her parents' wishes. So now what was the trouble with her!*, I wondered.

'What happened Naina? Everything OK?' my first words to Naina came out.

'No Aakash,' Naina replied.

'Tell me properly Naina, what has happened? Is anybody troubling you?' I again asked her.

'It's a clear case of dowry harassment Aakash,' Payal intervened.

'You mean... her in-laws...?' I asked.

'Yes,' Aarti said.

The office boy came with a tray containing four cups of coffee and biscuits. He placed the cups and the biscuit dishes carefully on the table and went.

'Naina, if you don't open up fully and tell me everything in detail, how will I know the case? How will I help you?' I asked her. Now I had to find it out.

Sliding a cup towards Naina, Aarti said to her, 'No need to be afraid or ashamed of anything Naina. We have come at the right place. Aakash is not only our friend, but now a lawyer too. Tell him everything, else how will he prepare for your case?'

I curiously looked at Naina, all ready to listen to her case. She let out a sigh and started with her case details.

'Aakash, as you know, I had an arranged marriage around four years back. His name is Daljeet Singh. They are a joint family staying in Santa Cruz. My parents had fully borne all my marriage expenses besides fulfilling all their demands which included cash, gold and a car. But still their wants didn't end,' Naina said as she took the first sip of her coffee. I could easily make out that her in-laws would have surely asked for more money. Aarti and Payal were quietly listening to Naina.

'Then?' I prodded.

'Now Daljeet wants to take a franchise of 3N Car Care, a reputed car servicing showroom chain, and for this he requires twelve lakh rupees. Instead of arranging it himself or taking it from his parents, he expects it from my father. He has been telling me to persuade my father to give him the amount to which I squarely refused him every time,' Naina continued.

'Have you informed about this to your parents?' I asked.

'Never! Even if I do, they, especially dad, would tell me to continue staying there and keep balancing the situation. So no point in telling them anything,' Naina replied. *Idiosyncrasy at its best*, I thought.

'Okay. What further?' I again prodded.

'He often hits me Aakash. On one pretext or the other, he has raised his hands on me ever since we got married. But this has increased a lot lately. Whenever he mentions about borrowing money from dad to start his business, I refuse him upfront. This enrages him and he beats me like anything,' Naina said with a heavy voice. I felt like detonating Daljeet with an explosive.

'Naina, tell him that incident also… he must know everything *na*? Payal whispered in her ears, loud enough for even me to hear.

'What happened Payal? I heard that,' I asked her. Maybe she could tell me.

'I'll tell it,' Naina said as she sniffed and continued, 'A few days back, Daljeet and his brother came to my room late at night. I was fast asleep. Must be one thirty or two, I don't remember properly. Daljeet woke me and initially abused me. Then he asked me to bring money from dad and give it to him in a week's time. When I protested, he first tried to strangulate my neck. His brother was a mute spectator to all this. They both were heavily drunk that night. When I was firm in my reply of not bringing a single penny from my parents, he…' Naina stopped and started to weep. With her face fully covered with her palms, she cried despondently. I didn't console her. First I wanted to know every single bit related to her case. Perhaps I was immune to the crying-and-consoling part of my clients.

I kept my head down till she finished weeping. 'I can't say anything further,' she said.

'Naina, tell him everything sweety. Let him know what those dogs have done with you,' Aarti intervened. But Naina, being from a middle-class conservative family, couldn't gather the courage needed to tell me what had happened that night.

With a choked tone, Naina continued, 'When I refused to budge, Daljeet removed his belt and started to whip me in front of his brother.'

Aarti and Payal looked at each other in disbelief. *Why on earth is she lying*, they wondered. Fearing that Payal may spill the beans, Naina clasped her hand hard under the table to prevent her from telling anything. Payal signaled Aarti to remain quiet with a slightest possible gesture. Naina never wanted to expose her marital rape in front of me. Maybe she was too embarrassed to tell it to me or that she never wanted it to come out in the court.

Naina's last sentence gushed the blood in my veins with a lightning speed. I clenched my teeth hard to avoid my emotions from coming out. *And you turned down my proposal to marry this guy*, I wanted to say. But how could I? She was technically my client at that moment plus I had to find out the whole story.

'Further?' I nudged her as I rested my chin on my palm.

'Then in a fit of rage, his brother whipped me too. I couldn't tolerate that. I started bleeding heavily and fell unconscious. Fearing adverse consequences, they admitted me to glory hospital and fled away. Nobody came to see me after that incident,' Naina finished her semi – fake ordeal with a heavy heart and red eyes.

I stood up from my chair and went towards the window. After pondering on her case for a while, I came back to my seat. 'So Naina, what do you want to do now?' I asked her.

'Teach him a lesson of his life,' came out an instant reply from Payal.

'Yes. They should be punished Aakash. We can't just let them go away like that…' Aarti added.

'That I understand Aarti. But the initiative has to come from Naina,' I said, looking right inside Naina's eyes. Though they were moist and red, they were still as beautiful as they were before.

'I've had enough Aakash. I have paid my price for marrying the one chosen by my parents. Nobody asked me my willingness for that man. But he violated all our marriage vows that night. I want to teach him a lesson of his life. And if need be, I'll go against my parents too if they create any hurdles in this. Send them a legal notice,' Naina said. Valiance had taken over on her. Payal and Aarti exchanged a satisfying smile with each other.

Naina's words filled my chamber with an air of positivity and enthusiasm. Never before had I seen her talk in such a way. But as they say, even a rocket doesn't soar up in space till its tail is put on fire!

'Okay. But one thing Naina, most important. Next time if you speak to Daljeet or any of his family members, shun all your feminism and respect. Talk to them as if you are going to eat them up any moment. You'll have to be thick – skinned from now on. They'll try to play with words or even threaten you or your family, but you don't budge. Here, based on your statement, I shall send them a notice tomorrow. You just stay tough. Leave the rest to me. Meanwhile, make a detailed written account of all the dates and events of whatever has happened with you. We'll need it further,' I said as the girls stood up to leave. It was almost 8:30 PM.

'The principal contents of your notice would be wrongful confinement, dowry harassment and mental and physical torture. Am I right?' I asked Naina.

'Can you ever been wrong Aakash?' Naina said as they exited my cabin.

***

'What the hell!' Tanvir Singh Khurana, Daljeet's father, exclaimed as he read Naina's notice to Daljeet. I had prepared it the same night and dispatched it next morning.

'Daljeet… what is all this?' Tanvir Singh said as he handed over Naina's notice to Daljeet.

Daljeet went berserk on reading the contents of the notice. 'What does she think of herself?' he murmured and removed his phone out of his pocket and dialed Naina's residence number.

'Hello,' Nisha answered the call.

'Give the phone to Naina,' Daljeet said in his characteristic ill-mannered tone.

Without saying anything, a furious Nisha banged the receiver on the table and stormed to Naina's room to call her. '*Didi*, Daljeet has called up. I think they have received your notice. Listen, no need to be afraid of them. Speak what you want to. If he goes overboard, just hang up. But no need to panic and all that OK,' Nisha advised her.

Naina nodded and came out of her room. 'Yes Daljeet?' she said.

'You bitch! How dare you –' Daljeet said as Naina interrupted him.

'Mind your language, you filthy dog. Once more you use a cuss word for me and I shall have you and your family thrown in a dungeon,' Naina attacked, for she was a cornered cat then.

Daljeet was taken aback on hearing Naina speak to him in that way. All along, she had been a dutiful wife who'd never even raise her voice for anything whatsoever. But today she was a free bird, at least pensively. And I had determined to make her a free bird lawfully too.

'Listen you… don't try to fly too high. It'll be better if you stay in your limits, otherwise –'

'Otherwise? Otherwise what? You will rape me again? And who will be your partner this time? You father?' Naina replied, akin to a man-eater who had tasted human blood.

'Shut up! Stop all this drama and come back by evening. And mind you, if you don't come, be ready to face the consequences,' Daljeet reprimanded.

'Oh, so you find all this a drama? You and your fucker brother raped me and threw me in the hospital and ran away… you find all this a drama Daljeet? Wait and watch, I'll not even touch you but remove all your clothes. See you in court now. No need to call back,' Naina said and banged the phone. Within moments, she realized that her entire face was in sweat.

'My school *wali didi* is back,' Nisha said and hugger her tightly.

'What happened?' Daljeet's father asked him.

'She doesn't want to come back,' Daljeet said.

'Look Daljeet,' Tanvir Singh said as he got up from his arm chair, 'we have bribed that inspector very heavily. Nobody comes out so easily in such cases. Remember, the police had come to arrest you and Harjot the very next day?'

'Yes, I remember. But this has to end somewhere, right? Now Naina wants to fight against me in court for such a small reason…' Daljeet thoughtfully enunciated.

'You feel it's a small reason Daljeet,' his mother intervened, 'But it isn't, in the eyes of law. You've manhandled her.'

'Go inside Gurpreet. Let us do the thinking part,' Tanvir Singh said. He was too bigot to allow women of the house to even opine in certain matters. Like always, the poor lady went inside without saying anything further.

'Look Daljeet, they are not going to keep quite now. Naina has gone to a lawyer and leveled heavy charges on you. At present she has only accused you of physical molestation and dowry demands. You have no option but to hire a lawyer and fight it out with her. If you remain silent, it'll seem like you agree to whatever she has alleged on you,' Tanvir Singh suggested.

***

A couple of days later, Tanvir Singh got the contact details of a lawyer named Advocate K. L. Dogra recommended by Amresh Singh, one of his old friends. 'He is a dynamic lawyer, very good in arguing cases in the court. Just go to him with Daljeet's case and give my reference,' he had said. Tanvir Singh passed on the contact details of the lawyer to Daljeet and Harjot and asked them to meet him at the earliest.

Advocate K. L. Dogra's office was situated on first floor of Laxman Commercial Plaza on Pedder Road. Daljeet and Harjot reached there at 11:00 AM sharp; they had taken his appointment over the phone the previous evening.

After attending three clients, Advocate K. L. Dogra called them in.

Advocate K. L. Dogra had a charming personality. He was well built, maybe in his late 20s and was heard to be a thorough professional. He gestured Daljeet and Harjot to sit, eyes still fixed on his laptop screen. A while later, he said, 'Yes, tell me.'

'Sir we have come from Santa Cruz. I am Daljeet and he is my brother Harjot,' Daljeet said as the lawyer shook hands with them.

'Tell me, what's the matter?' the lawyer came straight to the point.

'Sir, my wife has accused me and my family of troubling her with dowry demands. She has left the house and even sent us a legal notice,' Daljeet said as he handed over Naina's notice to the lawyer. Ignoring my name on my letterhead, Advocate K. L. Dogra went on to read it.

The moment he saw the name Naina on it, Advocate K. L. Dogra became alert. He scanned the entire notice carefully and asked, 'Tell me the background of your wife... like her parents, her family...'

'Sir they stay in Mahim, SBI staff quarters. Her father is a retired SBI manager and mother, a housewife. They –' he continued as Advocate Dogra stopped him.

'Wait a minute! Was she in Nathani Law College? Has she studied law?'

Daljeet gave a puzzled look to Harjot. 'No, I mean... I think I know her...' Advocate Dogra clarified.

'Yes, she is an LLB, but doesn't practice,' Daljeet said.

'Tell me everything,' Advocate Dogra said with a straight face.

In the next thirty minutes Daljeet and Harjot explained to him the entire scene which was completely fabricated. As strictly warned by their father, the brothers, akin to Naina, hid the rape incident and told the lawyer that whatever Naina had alleged on them was completely wrong. But a lawyer is a lawyer – he never sees who's at fault, rather he doesn't care. He'll only try to save his client, no matter what.

'I simply don't understand that if everything was going on smoothly, why did your wife leave your home all of a sudden and send you a charged notice Daljeet?' Advocate K. L. Dogra interrogated.

'Sir, all I wanted was to start a business. And Naina always wanted me to do a job as she belonged to a service – class family. My ambition to open my own car servicing showroom alone instigated her to take that step. She never believed my business acumen,' came out Daljeet's two-in-one reply - impressive but stupid! Advocate Dogra gave him a coy smile; he was qualified and experienced enough to judge the weight of Daljeet's reply.

'Anything else you are missing on?' he asked the duo.

'No Sir. We have told you everything. Remove us from

this mess. We'll pay you as much as you want,' the self-proclaimed future businessman, Daljeet Singh Khurana told the advocate.

'Hmm. Do one thing, in a day or two, give everything to me in writing. Prepare a detailed account on all the dates and events that have happened between you both. Remember, you have accused your wife with wrongful demands, picking up quarrels in small things, demanding excess money to buy things for her and so on, right? We have to falsify this in the court under all circumstances,' Advocate Dogra said.

'Sure Sir,' Daljeet said as he and Harjot got up to leave, 'By the way, how much will be your fees?'

'Prepare your written statement first, we'll discuss that later,' came out a smart reply from the smart lawyer.

Four days later…

'Bastards!' Naina's father cussed as he read Daljeet's notice.

'But what are they saying now? What's written in their notice Siddharth?' Naina's mother asked him.

'What will they say? They have leveled wrong charges against Naina. They are telling that Naina used to pick up quarrels over petty things, demanded unreasonable amounts from money from them and so on… here, read it,' Naina's father said as he hurled the notice to his wife.

She went through the entire notice, word to word and wondered, 'Oh God! What has happened all of a sudden? Everything was going smoothly till now… Now suddenly after four years of marriage –'

'Nothing was smooth, mummy,' Naina interrupted her mother, 'It was a horrible experience staying with those demons. Forget respect, I wasn't even treated as a human being. My own husband, who had taken seven vows with me, did what even an uneducated person doesn't do with his wife. I've been tortured, taunted and beaten all these years dad, but I never complained even once as I knew that you'd say that *it's all a part of married life.* But after that night's incident, I have become stronger and more competent. I shall fight it out with him in the court. I shall have my own share of justice, whether you are there with me or not.'

Naina's parents froze on hearing all this. A coy girl who always took care of the house, paid attention to her studies and never argued with her parents for anything eclipsed everyone today. A bad marriage had polished the crude diamond.

Naina read the entire notice. She immediately called me and informed everything. I asked her to stay calm and not to be deterred by such things as they were expected to happen. In a few days, I got the date of the first hearing of Naina's case in the Sessions Court. Neither I nor Advocate K. L. Dogra was aware that we were to come face to face in the court.

'Just be composed Naina, all we have is truth with ourselves. That'll alone help us to get justice for you,' is all what I had said to her.

7

First hearing of Naina Khurana v/s Daljeet Khurana case.

Sessions Court,
Kala Ghoda, Churchgate, Mumbai.

Judge – Justice Sunderlal Tripathi.

The day of the first hearing of Naina's case had arrived. I was more than ready with my case papers and arguments. Naina arrived in the courtroom at 11:30 AM sharp as was told to her. She was accompanied by her parents, Nisha, Aarti and Payal. Daljeet arrived after a few minutes along with Harjot. I mentally summarized all the points and kept my papers ready. The moment I turned to my left, I saw Daljeet's lawyer, Advocate K. L. Dogra. He was busy collating his case papers in his file, fully unaware that in a few minutes he will have to argue with me. I rubbed my eyes to believe myself: he was Kabir, Advocate Kabir L. Dogra. I looked at him, then at Naina. With a slight nod, I signaled her to look at Kabir. She was taken aback to discover Kabir in the court. Probably she couldn't realize that he was her opponent lawyer. Destiny had again brought us together – first in a law college, now in a court of law.

'Case no. 17, Naina Khurana.' Naina's name was announced as I kept my file on the table and got up from my chair. Bowing slightly to the presiding judge, Justice Sunderlal Tripathi, I introduced the case to him, 'My lord, my client Mrs. Naina Daljeet Khurana has filed a case against her husband, Mr. Daljeet Singh Khurana. The charges against him are mental and physical assault, dowry demands and unruly behavior by him and his family all the time. She hails from a middle-class family and her father had already given her in-laws a sizeable amount of stuff during their marriage. Still their demands didn't stop and they continued to pester her with bringing more from her parents, in pretext of which she was beaten, tortured and ill-behaved with. Naina has given a written statement detailing each and every incident. I request you to grant her justice, and nothing but justice my lord.'

Chills ran down Kabir's spine as he saw me. He couldn't believe that I was his opponent lawyer. Not that he was not equipped with fighting out with me; probably he never wanted to see either my or Naina's face as we both didn't go down well with him. Maybe he had a datum fixed in his mind that I was the culprit in Naina's rejecting his proposal.

'Your witness, please', Justice Sunderlal Tripathi turned to Kabir and said as he gingerly went through the case papers.

'My lord,' Kabir said as he got up, 'my client Mr. Daljeet Singh Khurana happens to be Naina's husband. I simply don't understand why Naina has to do all this whilst being married in one of the most respected and law abiding families of this city! The Khuranas stay as a joint family in the western suburbs and are well known for their gentle conduct in the society. I don't know what Naina will gain by defaming my client and his family; I only know that she has always been treated like a princess by the Khuranas. Now whether she wants to extract out money from them or wants a divorce, I don't know. I only know that my client is innocent and expect you to deter Naina from tarnishing my client's image. That's all, my lord.'

'Me lord, my client has been beaten and ill-treated by her husband and her in-laws ever since she has stepped in that house. Apart from bearing the entire marriage expenses, her father gifted some gold ornaments, some cash and even a car to her husband. This would have sufficed their needs, but I think getting satiated is not her husband's cup of tea. Now he wants to start his own business – a franchise of 3N Car Care, a car servicing showroom, for which he requires a capital of twelve lakh rupees. Instead of arranging for the sum by himself or asking his parents to help him out, Naina's husband has been pestering her to take it from her parents and give it to him,' I opened the case.

One-to-one murmurs ran across the court with the attendees ideating on their own. The judge signaled the court to be quiet in his characteristic *order – order* style with his hammer in his hand.

Kabir grinned. 'My lord, I think my friendly opponent sees two Hindi films a day,' he said as he got up. 'Nonetheless, I'd like to call Naina Khurana in the witness box,' he continued.

'Permission granted,' the judge said.

Naina got up and walked to the wooden, square shaped typical witness box placed a few feet away from the judge's chair. As a customary court ritual, the court peon came to her with a copy of The Holy *Bhagwadgita* wrapped in a red cloth in his hand and said, 'Place your hand on this and promise to speak the truth and nothing but the truth.'

Naina kept looking at the holy book before her for a few moments. Then turning towards the judge, she said, 'Sir, will the court believe in whatever I say if I touch the holy *Gita* and speak? Will my swearing on *Gita* be sufficient enough to punish my husband who has beaten me in front of God who exists in this *Gita*? But anyways, not to bother the court practice, I swear on *Gita* and promise that I shall speak the truth and nothing else.'

'So Naina, when did you marry Daljeet?' Kabir threw his first question to her.

'Four years back.'

'Was it a love marriage or an arranged marriage?'

'Arranged marriage.'

'Did you know Daljeet before marriage?'

'No, I didn't.'

'Well OK… what's so evil your husband did with you that you have dragged him to the court?'

'My husband and his family never treated me as a part of their family right from the beginning Sir,' Naina turned to the judge and replied, 'Not only they made me do every single household work, much like a maid servant, but also they ill-treated me and deliberately made me feel small.'

Kabir threw a bewildered expression at the judge and said, 'Me lord, what's the big deal if a lady does her household work? Would they be reduced to servants if they work in their own house? This is a ridiculous blame!'

Naina gave Kabir a piqued look. I gestured her to stay

calm.

'My lord, if there are two women in a house and only one is made to slog, things are bound to get unbalanced. Daljeet's brother Harjot is also married but his wife has stopped doing household chores ever since Naina has stepped in that house. What Naina meant was, she was made to do each end every work in that house without the responsibilities being shared fifty – fifty. And in return what did she get? Abuses? Physical torture, sometimes even assault? Harassment?' I argued.

'Harassment, as in?' the judge asked me.

'Objection my lord; my friendly opponent is trying to dig deeper without any reasonable cause. As I said earlier, Naina is a housewife who has a happy and satisfied married life. Now if she starts to malign the image of her in-laws, there will be no end to it. I think we should hit the target and finish this case as soon as possible to avoid her wasting the court's time,' Kabir intervened.

'Objection overruled,' the judge said.

'Thank you my lord,' I continued, 'What I said earlier may not be sufficient even to pay heed to, as in almost all the households women are made to do all the work. That's not a punishable crime and we are aware of it. But what made my client approach the court is the physical torture and harassment for dowry. While her husband needs to start his business, why should he depend on his father-in-law for its capital? Daljeet vexed Naina day in and day out so that she could bring twelve lakhs from her father, which is a sizeable figure out of the retirement fund of any service-class person. And when Naina was firm in not asking any amount from her parents, she was abused and frequently beaten. When all the limits were crossed, she was left with no choice but to return to her parents' house.'

'What limits my lord? Does a lady of a house fulfill her responsibilities or keep measuring various *limits* over there? I think now my opponent is trying to deflect the case elsewhere. There's no truth in my friendly opponent's statement. All they are trying to do is tarnish my client's image and cause trepidation to them for no apparent reason. Anyways, I'd like to call Daljeet in the witness box,' Kabir said.

'Permission granted.'

Daljeet stood up and walked towards the witness box. Everyone present in the court craned their neck to see him. He wore an ill-fitting jeans and an oversized shirt, tucked out. His shoes made a characteristic tip-toc sound as he walked towards the witness box. I saw him for the first time, wondering what made Naina marry a bozo like him!

'Swear on the *Gita* and promise to speak nothing but the truth,' the court peon said to him, extending the Holy *Gita*.

'I shall speak only the truth,' Daljeet said as he placed his palm on the *Gita*.

'Daljeet Singh, can you throw some light on the accusations of your wife on you?' Kabir asked him.

'What accusations my lord?' Daljeet said, turning towards the judge, 'I have always kept my wife with utmost dignity and respect. Neither I nor anybody from my family has ever done anything to her. But Sir, it was only after our marriage that I came to know her nature. She likes to pick up quarrels over petty things and blow things out of proportion for no apparent reasons. I tolerated all this as I know it is with almost all the women. But she demanded money every second day which I wasn't able to give her. She has a tendency for buying clothes for herself almost every week. Here I am trying hard to arrange for the capital for my new business but she is least bothered about it. All she is interested in is spending money on her clothes and other stuff.'

I stole a glance at Naina. She kept looking at Daljeet with teary eyes but a stern expression. In a moment, a drop of tear ran down her cheek. Realizing that she was standing in the witness box, she composed herself and wiped her tears with her bare hands.

'Mrs. Naina, your husband has a different story to say. Do you have to say anything in your defence?' the judge asked her.

'My lord, not even a single word of Daljeet is true. Now that I have dragged him to court, he is counter – allegating me. What he told is correct – he is trying really hard to arrange the money for his new business. But trying how? Did anybody ask him what efforts he is taking in arranging for the business capital? He is taking only one effort – pressing me to take it from my father. That's his only endeavor for it. I squarely refused him every time. When all his limits were stretched, he whipped me with his belt and left me bleeding. I got unconscious and was admitted to the hospital by him and his brother. Thereafter, nobody from his house came to see me or even check my whereabouts. I was lying lifeless in the hospital Sir,' Naina said as she started to weep. It's not every day that a petitioner is seen weeping in a witness box.

'My lord, Mrs. Naina may be asked that if she was beaten to the extent of admitting in a hospital, what were others doing in the house? Didn't anyone in their house try to stop Daljeet from beating her? And why wasn't anyone arrested?' Kabir asked the judge.

Shifting his spectacles upwards, the judge said, 'Mrs. Naina, you stayed in a joint family with your husband, right? So if the court were to believe your statement, why didn't anybody come forward to help you? Your father-in-law, mother-in-law, sister-in-law... everybody was asleep or what?'

Naina couldn't say anything further as she didn't want to disclose her marital rape in the court. Had she done so, she could have answered all the questions of the judge. She preferred to keep quiet.

'See Mrs. Naina, such allegations by women are common nowadays. Dowry harassment charges often lead to immediate arrests under section 498A. Sadly, this section is often used falsely against husband and his family by many women. I do not say that you are one of them, but your case and allegations seem too weak to proceed further. There's nobody who witnessed the incident you just told, inspite of so many members present in your house. Advocate Aakash, strengthen your case and bring a witness, mind you, a genuine one. I am giving a next date for this case. The court breaks for lunch now,' the judge announced as he stood up. Everybody followed suit.

'Don't worry, you'll be out in the next hearing,' Kabir said to Daljeet as they exited the courtroom.

***

I went to my office directly after the court hearing. *Something is missing*, my mind repeated inside me. Approaching a court was something a girl like Naina would opt as a last resort. I knew she was telling the truth. Or only half the truth. I just wanted to get justice for her.

Post lunch, I called up Naina. I had to talk to her as I wasn't convinced with the whole drama of the court today.

'Hi Naina, you back home?' I asked her.

'Yes Aakash.'

'Naina, drop in to my office this evening. I need to discuss this case further with you,' I said.

'Aakash, do you think we will be able to win the case?' Naina asked.

'You just come. Reach by six thirty. I'll finish all my appointments by then,' I said and hung up.

***

Naina reached at six thirty sharp; she was accompanied by Aarti. They were told to wait in the waiting area by my receptionist as I was busy with my client in my cabin. No sooner he left than I called them both in my cabin.

'Payal didn't come today…?' I asked. Maybe I felt like easening up the atmosphere.

'No, she had to attend to some guests today,' Aarti said.

'Okay. Look Naina, we are going on the right track, no doubt. But the charges that you have leveled on your husband and in-laws are too weak, at least to get them punished. A little dowry harassment here and there and they'll be put behind the bars… that doesn't happen so easily in our system. We have to prepare a water – tight case against them. And –' I said as I was interrupted by Aarti.

'Naina, I think it's about time you disclose the truth to Aakash. Listen babes, you are not going to lose anything. But if you hide the most important thing in the court, there's no meaning fighting out this entire thing,' Aarti said to Naina.

'Most important thing? What is it Aarti? Naina, did you hide anything from me?' I asked Naina, berserked.

Naina hung her head low. Aarti kept looking at her with an at least-tell-everything-now expression.

'What is it Naina?' I asked again. I was beginning to lose my patience.

Naina got up from her chair and went towards the window. Maybe she didn't want to meet my eyes. She kept gazing at the Doordarshan relay tower visible from my office. After a few moments she came back and took her seat. Eerie silence filled my cabin with me and Aarti waiting for Naina to speak up. Thousands of creepy thoughts started cropping up in my mind.

Aarti kept her hand on Naina's palm and gave her a comforting smile.

'Aakash, I've hidden the most important thing from you,' Naina said, looking at the bunch of files kept on my table.

'Wh… what?' I asked her, oscillating my eyes between her and Aarti. My heartbeats doubled every passing moment.

'This is the incident of the night when I was admitted to glory hospital. Daljeet and Harjot got heavily drunk and entered my room. I was fast asleep. Daljeet woke me up and asked whether I would bring money from my parents or not. I refused him, as usual. In his intoxication and hunger for more money from my parents, he strangulated my neck, almost to the point of asphyxiating me. Till here, I told you the last time. But the real truth that followed this is something else,' Naina said.

I didn't utter a word. I wanted the silence of my cabin to push her to talk.

'I screamed as loudly as I could. Hariram, our servant woke up and knocked the door of my room. Harjot didn't allow him to enter the room and somehow got rid of him. When I told Daljeet that he ought to arrange the capital by himself instead of begging from my parents, he did what even a monster cannot do,' Naina continued.

'What did he do Naina? You said he whipped you with his belt…' I said.

'No. If that would have been the case, perhaps I wouldn't

be sitting here today. Aakash…' Naina said as her eyes were filled with tears to the brim.

'Hey… what happened Naina?' I said as I got up and went to her, 'Please tell me the entire thing. And listen, you don't have to be scared of anyone okay.'

'Aakash, when I did not give in to his demands, he raped me. He raped me Aakash, right in front of Harjot. And as if this weren't enough, even Harjot raped me after Daljeet,' Naina said and started weeping miserably.

I stood still before Naina. I couldn't believe my ears. My head started spinning. I, however, composed myself and took my seat.

Naina wept and wept as Aarti kept consoling her. I allowed her to ease up for some time. Meanwhile, I ordered tea for all of us.

'I am listening Naina,' I said after a few moments.

Naina continued, 'I was in my menses that night. Though they used a protection, I still couldn't bear the heinous acts of Daljeet and Harjot. I fell unconscious and started bleeding. Fearing serious consequences, they took me to glory hospital and dumped me over there. They even filled wrong contact details in the hospital admission form. After that, neither Daljeet nor anybody from his family came to the hospital or even contacted me, except when Daljeet threatened me over the phone to take my case back a few days ago.'

I was completely shattered on hearing all this. A husband raping his wife in front of his own brother and even allowing him to rape her! This was the most challenging case I had come across in my law career. But before being judgmental, I had to know the entire story.

'Sorry to hear all this Naina,' I said, 'Is there anything else you would like to say?'

'Yes. That night I was examined by the gynecologist and rape was confirmed, looking at my condition and going by my statements. The hospital authorities immediately informed the police. Next day, a constable came and took my statement. Daljeet and Harjot were arrested immediately, but their father Tanvir Singh heavily greased the palms of the inspector investigating this case and soon they were set free. So all this made me approach a lawyer, who incidentally turned out to be you,' Naina narrated her ordeal. Her eyes had turned dry by now. Or was it just my imagination? Who knows?

'Aakash Sir, tea,' my office boy said as he softly knocked the door of my cabin.

'Yeah, come in,' I said. He placed the tea cups with a plate of biscuits and went. 'Anything else, Naina?' I asked her, shifting her tea cup towards her.

'That's what has actually happened Aakash. I... I am sorry I didn't tell all this in the very beginning. Actually, I should have. But...'

'I understand Naina. But in legal battles we need to keep our feelings aside and stick to the truth, isn't it?' I said.

'Hmm.'

'So Aakash, what next? Won't the judge say that now we are digressing the case somewhere,' Aarti said as she took the first sip of her tea.

'We just need to speak the truth in the court, what else?' I replied, almost immediately.

'Look Naina, whatever you've faced, speak it up before the judge baby. Let the truth be known to everybody. Daljeet has to be punished under any circumstances. That was our only motto in approaching the court, isn't it? No point in telling half truth and hiding the other half,' Aarti said to Naina.

'Naina, Aarti is right. Our next date is only a few days away. Whatever you've told me today, you should have told me on the very first day when you had come here. Nevertheless, now don't hide anything in the court, however cruel and maligning it may be. Remember Naina, we have only one tool in the court - our truth,' I said.

8

Second hearing of Naina Khurana v/s Daljeet Khurana case.

Sessions Court,
Kala Ghoda, Churchgate Mumbai.

Judge – Justice Sunderlal Tripathi.

'Me lord, my client Mrs. Naina Daljeet Khurana has something more to say today. What she told us last time was true, but she hid the most appalling fact in fear of disreputation of her and her family. A fact that is going to shake this court today. I would like to mention it to the court, with your permission,' I said.

'Permission granted,' the judge said.

'My lord, in the last hearing, Naina told the court that her husband and his brother got drunk that night and asked her to bring money from her parents to start their own business. Like always she opposed him so he tried to strangulate her. The story remains a fact till here. After that, she wasn't whipped by her husband, he did worse. He raped her right in front of his brother. Post that, he asked his brother Harjot too to rape her. Naina couldn't tolerate it as she was in her menses. She started bleeding and fell unconscious. Fearing dire consequences, her husband and his brother admitted her to glory hospital and fled from there,' I narrated the most dreadful incident from Naina's life to the judge right in front of fifty-some people present in the court.

Murmurs ran across the length and breadth of the court. Everybody started looking at Naina on hearing a new story about her. The very fact that people change their perception about a raped woman in a jiffy is something worth researching. My statement had violently shaken Kabir from within. He had no idea what was going on. Maybe he thought that this was just my game to win the case in any circumstances. However, he kept his cool and signaled Daljeet and Harjot to remain calm.

The judge gave a cursory look at Naina's case papers. 'Then why did your client give a false information in the last hearing?' he asked me.

'She didn't want this to come out in the court my lord. No ordinary housewife would like to get herself exposed to this limit. But now that she has spoken the truth, I request you to consider this incident and further this case,' I requested the judge.

'Mrs. Naina, please come in the witness box,' the judge said.

Naina just couldn't move from her chair. All eyes were glued to her. Maybe she anticipated some dreaded questions by the judge. Payal somehow coaxed her to get up and go to the witness box.

'Mrs. Naina, your lawyer claims that you were raped by your husband and his brother that night. Is it correct?' the judge asked her.

'Yes Sir, it is.'

'Then why didn't you admit it in the first hearing?'

'Sir, I never wanted all this to come out in the court. I feared that it would malign my family's image in society,' Naina said.

'Then why are you saying it in this hearing? Won't it damage your family's social image now?' the judge asked her.

'Had I not done so, my husband would have walked free, all thanks to our law and order machinery which runs solely on proofs and evidences,' Naina said.

'Let us not worry about the working of our law and order madam. Please stick to your case and especially, your statements. Nonetheless, the court would like to know what has turned you into a rebel against your husband after four years of marriage,' the judge retorted.

'Sir, I was never treated as a part of their family right from the inception of my marriage. Even in trivial things my husband used to raise his hands on me right before his parents. I used to slog from dawn to dusk to keep my husband and my in-laws happy. But what did I get in return? Nothing! No love, no respect, no position in the family. I wasn't even allowed to speak in their family matters.

As if all this weren't enough, I was subjected to verbal and even physical torture at times for no apparent reason. Initially I thought it was me who lacked in some things... that I wasn't able to live up to their expectations. As time flew by, I realized that the main cause of their unruly behavior was their unquenched thirst for more money from my parents...'

'Objection, my lord. I would like to cross examine her,' Kabir intervened.

'Objection overruled,' the judge said.

Naina continued, 'My husband wanted to start his own car servicing showroom for which he required a capital of twelve lakhs. When he failed in his attempts to convince me to bring it from my parents, he resorted to violence. He thought that hitting his wife might prove his manliness. I tolerated all his torments in a hope that someday he would realize his mistakes. But there was no end to it. That night, he and his brother got drunk and they both raped and dumped me to the hospital and fled from there. When they were there in my room, their servant Hariram listened to my screams and came to my room asking for me, but was somehow got rid of by Harjot. This man, who had taken seven vows with me never even bothered to find out whether I was alive or dead. I'm sorry Sir; I should have mentioned these facts in the very first hearing itself. But women like me are always in close quarters with disparagement.'

Acute silence filled the otherwise usually chirpy and noisy courtroom. The transcriptor was busy making his notes of Naina's statements. Everybody present in the court went dead silent, perhaps waiting for the judge to speak. Today I cursed Naina's destiny – a girl who couldn't even accept my proposal in college in the fear of her parents had narrated her ordeal standing in the witness box of a court.

'Advocate Kabir, do you have any questions?' the judge asked Kabir.

'Yes me lord,' Kabir said as he stood up and went to Naina, 'Mrs. Naina, you say that your husband and his brother raped you and all that. OK, fine. So why didn't the hospital inform the local police?'

'They did. The same night. They both were arrested the very next day as I told last time. But as they bribed the inspector, they were soon let free.'

'Good! What's the name of the doctor who treated you?'

'Dr. Sulbha Sareen, visiting gynaecologist in glory hospital.'

'Very good! Why did you not go to the local police again to find out whether they were in police custody or not?' Kabir threw his third question.

'The Khuranas were hand in glove with the police inspector. Before the matter could spring up, they greased his palms and were soon let fee. And thanks to lawyers like you that people like me have to stand in witness boxes and answer to dumb questions like these,' Naina replied.

'No personal remarks, please,' the judge intervened.

'OK Mrs. Naina, tell me one thing, your four year-long marriage doesn't bear a child. Why?' Kabir asked Naina.

'Objection, my lord. This has nothing to do with this case. Whether my client has a child or not, how does that matter to my friendly opponent?' I screamed at more than my usual tone.

'It matters. It matters, my friend,' Kabir replied, looking at me, 'I just want to prove how far your client can go to mislead the court.'

'What do you mean by *your client is misleading the court*? Can't you see her pain? Can't you realize that she has put her prominence at stake just for the sake of justice?' I shouted at Kabir.

'Order, order,' the judge horned in, only to fall on deaf ears.

'Of course she is misleading the court. Firstly she said that her husband whipped her with a belt that night. Now today she says that he and his brother raped her. Now in the third hearing she might say that she was forced into prostitution by her in-laws in greed of more money,' Kabir threw a random argument.

'How dare you say that Kabir? You are maligning my client's image. You better apologise to her. Right now, before I prepare a new case against you,' I howled at Kabir at thrice my volume. Everybody got up from their chairs to have a better view of two lawyers fighting like mad dogs.

'Order, order,' the judge keyed in again, 'I am sitting here. No need to be judgmental. And advocate Kabir, please stick to the case.'

'Pardon me, my lord. But that's exactly what I am doing. I only want to prove that Mrs. Naina wants to, on one pretext or the other, get her husband punished for no perceptible reason. She's coming up with newer stories every time, nothing else. Otherwise how would the police let her husband and his brother go, who were charged with raping her? How is it possible that nobody apart from their servant Hariram listened to her screams that night? People in that house were sleeping, not dead. Then how come nobody came for her help? And most important of all, there is no servant by the name Hariram in that house! My lord, this isn't a case, this is just a waste of time,' Kabir argued. Maybe he wanted to defeat me anyhow simply because Naina was involved in this case.

'No my lord, there is a case. A very strong case. Naina's mouth was stuffed with a cloth, hence she couldn't scream. Then how do we expect anybody to come to her rescue? Secondly, whom are we expecting a help from? Her in-laws? Who were least bothered about her all these years…?! Even if they would have listened to her screams, I am sure nobody amongst them would have come to help her,' I cross argued.

'I differ to this, my lord. The Khuranas are amongst the most respected people in society. They do not have enmity with anyone. On the contrary, they have helped a lot of people. I think there's no meaning in beating around the bush. My client is not guilty and that's a fact,' Kabir said, throwing his hands up in air.

'After listening to both the sides of this case, this court charges Daljeet Singh Khurana and his brother Harjot Singh Khurana not guilty. Mrs. Naina Daljeet Khurana may be given to understand that none of her statements are valid enough to proceed with this case. But if she wants to, her lawyer, Advocate Aakash will have to produce a witness within two weeks time, in failure of which this case shall be dismissed. This court also instructs Mumbai police department to probe whether the police officer in question had taken a bribe and let Daljeet Singh and his brother Harjot Singh free. Next case please,' the judge declared.

A collective wave of disappointment ran across the courtroom. I stood still before the judge, for his judgment solely depended on the presence of proofs and witnesses for any case. Our law and order machinery heavily relies on witnesses, no matter what may be the truth, so much so that even an innocent lady pleading for justice wasn't granted one.

Naina was flocked by her parents, her sister Nisha, Aarti and Payal with each one of them trying to console her. We had almost lost the case. Hell, I couldn't even help Naina get justice. Daljeet and Harjot exited the courtroom along with Kabir. I went back to my seat, feeling defeated for the first time. But my other half held on to me as I knew that Naina wasn't lying. She deserved her own share of justice.

That night I decided to meet Kabir regarding this case. I wanted to have the cake and eat it too. I just shot him a text –

hi kabir
wanna catch up wid u
2mrw morning, my ofce?

I wasn't sure whether I did the right thing by texting him; I just wanted to make him realize that he was helping wrong people and denying justice to Naina which was her moral and legal right.

I couldn't wait for the next day.

9

My phone beeped of an incoming message the next day. It was Kabir's reply to my previous night's message –
Whats d matter? y u wnt 2 meet me?
I replied –
Dis is imp. Pls drop in 2 my ofce.
He wrote –
Y, u afraid of losing the case or wat??? Nywayz, I don't hav tym...
I replied –
Nothing like dat. It concerns an innocent life. Pls spare an hour & come 2 me.
He wrote –
Wl b der @ 10.

I reached my office at 9:30 AM, half an hour before my usual time and cancelled all my morning appointments till noon. I made a note of all the points, important and trivial, related to Naina's case to be discussed with Kabir. I only wanted to make him realize that he was providing a shell to the wrong people. Losing the case was the last thing in my mind.

Kabir arrived at ten sharp at my office. My receptionist told him to come directly to my cabin as was instructed to her. The moment he entered my cabin, I got up from my chair and extended my hand for a handshake. With raised eyebrows, he shook his hand gingerly and asked, 'Why have you called me here?'

'What will you have? Tea or coffee?' I asked him.

'Tea is fine,' he said as he scanned my whole cabin. I think he mentally admired it.

I summoned my office boy to get tea for both of us. 'Thanks for coming Kabir,' I said.

'That's alright. But why me here?' he asked again.

I took a deep breath and said, 'Look Kabir, firstly please understand that my calling you here has a genuine reason. It concerns a life. Secondly, please don't think that I want to be arm in arm with you and drag Naina's case forever in the court and keep making money from it. I think it's high time we should know whom we are helping before it's too late.'

'I don't quite understand that... will appreciate if you come straight to the point,' Kabir said.

'Well, I am talking about Naina's case. Beyond doubt, you are doing your duty as a lawyer and protecting your client. And let me admit, you are doing good. But I guess we both know who's right and who's at fault in this case.'

'I see! So you want me to either leave this case or lose it, yeah?' Kabir asked.

'No ways Kabir. Your presence is much needed in this case. Being a lawyer, your arguments stand valid at every point, but they are gradually pushing Naina towards a black hole from where she won't be able to probably return one day,' I clarified.

'So what do you want me to do then? Chicken out of this case...?' an inquisitive Kabir asked.

Just then, my office boy arrived with a tray containing two tea cups and a plate of cashew cookies. He placed the cups on the table, each before us and the cookies plate in the center and left.

'I know the reality Kabir. And trust me, every word of her is true to its core. She hasn't fabricated anything in her statements. But –' I said as he interrupted me.

'Every lawyer thinks that his client is speaking the truth Aakash. So what? Even I claim that my client is not lying. So let us fight it out in the court and see who's guilty. We'll only waste each other's time here,' Kabir said and got up to leave.

'Wait Kabir, let the lawyer within us not kill the human inside us. My intention is not to convince you about Naina, it's just that we both have to proceed in the right direction,' I said, blocking his way.

'So basically you want to say that Naina is telling the truth and Daljeet is lying? OK. So what? Let the court decide who's right and who's wrong. You do your part and I'll do mine. Simple!'

'Kabir, it may be too late then,' I said in a sunken tone, 'We both were in love with her at some point of time. She had rejected our proposals only to marry as per her parents' wish, remember?

She fulfilled her duties as a daughter, thereafter as a daughter-in-law. And today when she needs our help, we are relying on the witness-based law and order system to salvage her? Is it just Kabir? Think *yaar…*'

Kabir went silent. Maybe he had nothing to argue further. I kept looking at him with some hope in my eyes that he would cooperate with me to remove Naina from the mess she had been living in. He quietly sipped his tea, looking outside the window.

'So what do you want me to do? Shall I leave this case then?' he finished his tea and asked me in a gentle tone. For the first time in my life he spoke to me in a placid manner.

'No!' I replied and went to sit next to him, 'As I said earlier, you are required to be there for this case. And let me assure you again Kabir, every word spoken by Naina is true. She has been manhandled ever since she stepped in that house. Getting thrashed for no reasons was an everyday affair for her. She has faced a lot of harassment as she was resolute in not bringing money from her parents to give to Daljeet. And what did that bastard do? He raped her right before his brother and allowed him to rape her too. They then dumped her in the hospital when they saw her bleed. For name sake they were arrested, but they bribed the cop and walked out free. Now tell me Kabir, did Naina deserve all this? Forget about witnesses or proving anything in the court…'

Acute silence filled my cabin. Kabir was lost in his own thoughts. Finally after some contemplation, he spoke. 'What to do now?'

'See Kabir,' I said, 'I alone won't be able to give justice to Naina. I need your help in this.'

'What kind of help?' Kabir asked.

'I exactly don't know. But we have to do something without being obvious. For now, if I change my course of track or you yours, it might come in the eyes of the judge or even the Khuranas. So whatever has to be done, it has to be discreet,' I suggested.

'That's true. But how do we begin?' Kabir asked.

'First and foremost, we need to excavate all the details of Daljeet Singh and his entire family for the past several years. I don't think even you know that… I mean… you only know what he has told you till date. Nothing beyond that,' I said.

'And are we equipped to do all this? I doubt…' Kabir said.

I went silent. *Now who the hell will dig out all their details*, I thought. Next moment, I came up with a bizarre idea.

'Kabir… let's hire a private detective for this.'

'What? A detective!' Kabir exclaimed with raised eyebrows.

'I think there are a lot of things about the Khuranas that we don't know. My gut feeling says that. I may be completely wrong, but it'll be worth the effort.'

Kabir pondered over my idea for a few moments. I waited for his reaction. 'And what if we come to know that they aren't nice people?' Kabir asked.

'If ever it is true, we shall teach them a lesson they'll never forget. They have miserably played with someone's life Kabir. We won't spare them. Naina doesn't deserve all this,' I said. I think my words worked this time.

'You are right. Let's search some private detectives online. Can I use your laptop?' Kabir said after mulling over my statement.

'By all means!' I said as I shifted my laptop towards him. He logged on to the website of Justdial and searched for some good private detectives in Mumbai. He got twelve results. He started going through the reviews of the clients of each agency. After reading for around fifteen minutes, he said, 'Aakash look, I think I've found one.'

I craned my neck towards the laptop screen to have a better view. 'It's Blue Panther detective agency run by one Mr. Prakash Rajput, an ex-serviceman,' Kabir said. We went through the entire website, their history, their success ratio and most important of all, the reviews of their clients. Everything seemed perfect.

Blue Panther detective agency was operational in Mumbai since 2001. It had only one office in Tardeo, Mumbai Central with a team of fifteen private detectives – twelve men and three women. The website showed only their pseudo names, no correct names, mobile numbers or photographs were displayed over there. The only contact number available was the direct number of their head, Mr. Prakash Rajput.

Kabir took out his phone from his pocket and dialed

Prakash's number. He answered his call after two rings, 'Hello!'

'Hello, may I speak with Mr. Prakash Rajput?' Kabir said.

'Prakash here. Who's calling?'

'Mr. Prakash, I am Advocate Kabir Dogra from Worli. I need your appointment for an urgent case that I am handling.'

'OK. My office is in Tardeo. You can drop in between four and five today. After five, I will be out,' Prakash said.

'Can I drop in right now, if it is OK with you?' Kabir asked.

'One moment, you said you are calling from Worli, right?' Prakash said.

'Yes.'

'Right now I am in Prabhadevi. Will finish my work in the next ten minutes. En route my way to office, I can drop in at yours,' Prakash said.

'Even that will suit me. It's my friend, Advocate Aakash Khanna's office. I'll text you the address right away. It's bang opposite Sasmira,' I said.

'Sure. I'll be there by eleven thirty,' Prakash said and hung up.

'He'll be here in the next twenty minutes,' Kabir said as he texted my office address to Prakash.

'Kabir, I don't have words to thank you man… I never expected that you'd cooperate with me to this extent,' I said as Kabir pressed the *send* button.

'Don't thank me Aakash. We both are selflessly doing this for someone else. Naina is a victim and everybody, including the judge, knows this. Even I knew it in the first hearing itself. But we are no judges; we just have to stick to the legal protocols and save our clients, that's it. But your calling me here today is an eye-opener for me. So for this case, we'll have to bend the rules but still continue playing the game,' Kabir said. I gave him a thumbs up.

'One more thing,' Kabir said, 'Don't disclose anything to Naina as of now. Let's first see the report of Blue Panther.'

'Sure!'

***

Detective Prakash Rajput arrived at 11:45 PM. My

receptionist asked him to directly come to my cabin as was instructed to her. He softly knocked the door of my cabin and said, 'Advocate Kabir Dogra?'

Kabir turned to him and realized at once that he was Prakash. He got up from his chair and said, 'Yes, Mr. Rajput, please come in.' Prakash followed suit.

Detective Prakash Rajput had a charismatic personality. He wore a denim blue jeans shirt complimented with charcoal black corduroy pants. His hair was well combed and short, a characteristic feature of all defence personnel, retired or in service. After a firm handshake with both of us, he took his seat. 'Yes Mr. Dogra, how can I help you?' he said to Kabir.

'Mr. Rajput, we have a case with us. It concerns a lady. Though we are opponent lawyers in this case, we need to collectively work at this stage to find out a few things. And for that we need yours and your team's help,' Kabir said to him.

'Okay. What exactly do you want me to do?' he asked. I summoned my office boy for three cups of coffee.

In the next ten minutes, Kabir briefed him everything related to Naina's case. Prakash listened to him with rapt attention.

'You said you are Daljeet's lawyer, right? And you yourself want to put him at risk!' Prakash said, tilting his left eyebrow a bit upwards.

'We are, and will continue to be opponent lawyers. But only in court. We both know that Naina is innocent. We just want to get her justice legally. And for that, we shall work in liaison outside the court,' I stepped in.

'Two opponent lawyers working for the same cause? I am impressed!' Prakash said.

'It's much needed Mr. Rajput, otherwise there will be a big blunder by the hands of law,' Kabir said.

'OK fine. Give me all the available details of Daljeet Singh Khurana and his family on a paper. Provide as much details as you can. Rest, I and my team will find out,' Prakash said.

I and Kabir prepared a write up of all the details of the Khuranas as much as we knew and gave it to Prakash. 'It will take maximum ten days,' he said as he went through it.

'We need to find out everything about them. That will decide our next course of action. We don't want him to walk free and deny justice to Naina. Hope you understand Mr. Rajput,' I said with some hope in my voice.

'Don't worry. We'll unearth all their past and present details and prepare a confidential report. It'll surely help you in the court,' Prakash said as he got up to leave.

'We'll call you after ten days for the report,' I said.

'You may not, as we might complete our work before that. And one more thing...' Prakash said as I and Kabir looked at each other.

'Call me Prakash,' he winked as he exited my cabin.

10

Blue Panther detective agency commenced its work from the next day itself. Prakash chose three detectives for this case and gave them all the information about the Khuranas. The trio sprang in action and began their work by first putting the Khuranas' house under surveillance. Their job was to find out all the past details of Daljeet Singh as regards his profession, personal life, character, enmity, call records and so on. Detectives of Blue Panther agency were known to work so discreetly that they could not seem obvious even in a CCTV footage! They had their own informers as well. Prakash took a daily report from them and began to prepare a confidential report. In eight days flat, everything regarding the Khuranas was on papers. Prakash called Kabir and informed him the same. Kabir asked him to come to his office with the report the next day.

Prakash reached Kabir's office the next day at ten in the morning. 'So Prakash… what does your confidential report say?' Kabir asked him.

'I haven't come across such a frenzied guy all throughout my career! You'll be shocked to know his details,' Prakash said.

'Really? Can I see the report?' Kabir asked.

'All yours!' Prakash said as he handed over the 60-paged report to Kabir. I went next to him to have a look at the report.

'What do the findings say?' I asked Prakash.

'A lot. Let me verbally tell you about Daljeet Singh. He is what he doesn't show. He has hidden a lot of things from Naina and her family, and from you as well Kabir,' Prakash said.

Kabir suddenly closed the report file and kept it on the table. 'Tell us everything Prakash,' he said.

'Daljeet Singh Khurana and his family are extremely money-minded people. They can go to any extent to siphon money off anyone. This fact came to my attention when I learnt that Daljeet was initially married to his brother Harjot's wife's sister,' Prakash said.

'What? Daljeet was married before he got married to Naina?!' I asked Prakash with twice my volume. Kabir fumbled for words as this came as a big blow to him too.

'Yes. Harjot Singh's wife Lovleen had a younger sister who was married to Daljeet in 2007. But she committed a suicide somewhere in December 2008,' Prakash said.

'Suicide? Why?' Kabir asked.

'Well, the story dates back to 2007 when Daljeet got married to Lovleen's sister Simran. Simran Kaur Bhatti. All went well for the first three to four months. But soon, Daljeet started demanding money from her parents to upgrade his business. They gave him around three lakhs to upgrade his motor garage which he had in Sion Koliwada. But not a single pie from this was used in business upgradation; he spent all that money on his own expenses, mostly being drinks. Whenever Simran used to ask him about those three lakhs, Daljeet used to silence her by hitting her,' Prakash opened the first chapter of Daljeet's life.

I and Kabir looked at each other in disbelief. 'This is just the beginning,' Prakash said.

'Then?' I asked as I rested my chin on my right palm.

'After somewhere around eight months, Daljeet again asked for money from Simran's parents. This time, Simran was resolute in not asking money from her parents. She squarely refused Daljeet and told him to concentrate on his business and not idle away his time. This enraged Daljeet who beat her with his belt. Everybody could hear her screams but nobody came to her help,' Prakash said.

'Even Lovleen didn't stop all this? She was Simran's elder sister after all…' I interrupted.

'Yes and no. Lovleen's parents had adopted Simran from an orphanage when she was two. Right from childhood, Lovleen had a strange kind of hatred for Simran. Simran was gifted with immense beauty and a rational thinking ability, which Lovleen wasn't. But everything got washed off the day she got married to Daljeet. Hence Lovleen didn't interfere when Daljeet was unjust to Simran. Instead, she enjoyed it,' Prakash said.

Prakash's words came to me like hot balls of fire being tossed on me, one after the other. *This isn't a time to react, there's more to come*, I said to myself and continued to listen to him.

'But what made her commit suicide?' Kabir asked.

'One evening, after her usual thrashing session from Daljeet, Simran closed the door of her room and locked it from inside. Everyone in the house had been to *langar* at a nearby Gurudwara. Simran couldn't take more of what life gave her after marriage. She cursed herself; she couldn't find a way to get out from there. That evening she hanged herself by her dupatta from the ceiling fan of her room. She was generous enough to not leave a suicide note hence Daljeet was arrested only as a formality. Nothing could be proved against him in the court, hence he walked free,' Prakash said.

'Son of a bitch! Couldn't believe myself that I was helping this person…' Kabir murmured.

'Aakash, did you ask Naina why she didn't have a baby in almost four years of her marriage?' Prakash asked me.

'Actually, no. I…' I said as Prakash interrupted me.

'You guys will be shocked to know that Daljeet is a sterile man. He cannot bear a child. That's why they didn't, rather couldn't have a family in four years of their marriage. And Daljeet knew this after he got married to Simran. But he and his family hid this fact from Naina's parents,' Prakash revealed the obvious.

'But how did Daljeet come to know about his sterility?' Kabir asked him.

'After Daljeet's marriage with Simran, he wanted a child. They tried for a year but to no avail. Simran's gynaecologist initially advised Daljeet to undergo a sperm count and sperm motility test. The sperm count test results were negative, which means Daljeet's sperm count was OK but his sperms lacked the requisite motility. Simran too underwent the required tests for fertility. All her test reports were normal. Even after a medication of two years, Daljeet's results remained the same. Hence he couldn't bear a child with Simran. Same story was repeated with Naina; their four year-old marriage couldn't bless them with a child,' Prakash said.

'I have no words to say… how can a person be so cruel,

irrational and inhuman, all at a time?' I said.

'This means, Daljeet and his family has cheated on Naina. Big time!' Kabir added.

'Daljeet shut down his Koliwada's motor garage a while back as all the mechanics left their work. He didn't pay them regularly so they started working elsewhere. Now he wants to take a franchise of 3N Car Care for which he needs twelve lakhs. So he has been pestering Naina to arrange this amount from her parents. All that led her land in hospital and thereafter, her home. These are the call records, details of his past business, photocopy of his and Simran's wedding invitation card and his character report. Mind you guys, confidential reports of Blue Panther detective agency hold water in Metropolitan Magistrate Court, Sessions Court and even in High Court,' Prakash said, concluding his report verbally.

Kabir took the report file in his hands. Now it was our tool to proceed in the right direction. He handed the file to me. I flipped its pages, each telling me a new story of how a man could play not only with his own life, but with others' too.

'What are your charges Prakash?' I asked.

'Twenty six thousand six hundred, including service tax.'

'Can we pay it by two cheques?' Kabir asked him. I and Kabir had already decided to pay him fifty-fifty.

'Will do. The cheque should be in favour of Blue Panther detective agency. I shall also email you the soft copy of this report by evening,' Prakash said.

I and Kabir wrote two cheques of Rs. 13,300 each and handed them to Prakash.

'Thank you! And wish you good luck for this case,' Prakash said as he left.

'Can't believe I was defending Daljeet! He's a murderer. He's a traitor. He may not have killed his first wife, but is fully responsible for her death. Poor girl had no other option but to hang herself. Imagine what all she and Naina must have gone through while staying with him!' Kabir wondered.

'I told you in the very beginning Kabir, Naina isn't lying. The day she narrated her case to me, I don't know why but I could gauge that she was speaking the truth. And when I saw Daljeet for the first time in the court, his face itself said it all. Wonder what made Naina marry a person like him!' I said.

'She's amongst those girls of our society who do everything as per their parents' wish Aakash. Nothing much can be done in this. Nonetheless, where do we head now? Prakash has opened up everything before us,' Kabir said.

'We have several ways to deal with this case now. At least I have this report in my hand,' I said, pointing out to the confidential report file given by Prakash, 'However, with a strong defence lawyer like you, it would take ages for this case to reach any conclusion.'

'That's exactly what I am thinking Aakash. I think we'll have to weaken one side of this case all by ourselves. Only then we'll be able to navigate in a defined direction,' Kabir enunciated.

'Weaken… as in?' I asked.

'I don't know… maybe we'll have to strategize a few things in this case. Because in both the hearings, my arguments stood valid. It doesn't mean yours didn't, the only thing that matters here is a concrete evidence needed by the court. Of course, this report is going to help us big time, but in addition to it we need a certain game plan here,' Kabir explained.

'I think deliberately weakening this case will help us. We need to push things gradually in Naina's favour. But Kabir, Naina is *my* client. You understand… you'll have to lose this case then…' I said.

'I am not concerned about winning or losing here. I am sure, neither you are. We just want Naina to get justice, that's it.'

'So what's the game plan? I shall produce this report in the court at the right moment and argue accordingly. You keep weakening your statements and slowly drift the case in Naina's favour. Also, you'll be required to baselessly argue at times,' I ideated.

'Seems perfect. This is the only option to save Naina. I'll be happy to lose this case if Naina gets justice by our strategy,' Kabir said. For the first time in my life I adored him from the bottom of my heart.

'Kabir, prior to all this, I think we should inform everything about Daljeet to Naina and her parents, shouldn't we?' I asked.

'I was about to tell you that. That'll all the more help us steer in the right direction. It will also avoid miscommunication,' Kabir said.

I nodded and took out my phone and dialed Naina's number. She answered after three rings.

'Hello?'

'Naina, Aakash here. Can we talk?' I said.

'Yes Aakash,' Naina replied in a pensive tone.

'Naina, I want you to come to my office along with your parents,' I said.

'Huh… what?' a perplexed Naina asked me.

'Yes, you heard it right. Drop in to my office this evening by six. Bring uncle and aunty along with you. If possible, Nisha too.'

Naina couldn't figure out my calling her parents to my office. 'You don't worry about the fee part, I'll pay it as –' she said as I interrupted her.

'It has nothing to do with my fees Naina; please don't embarrass me. I need to inform you and your parents something important pertaining to Daljeet. It will help us in the court.'

Naina went silent. She couldn't speak anything further. She just agreed to visit my office with her parents the same evening and kept the phone.

'Kabir,' I said, 'thank you!'

'Anything for justice, junior,' he winked.

11

'But why does he want to meet us all of a sudden?' Naina's father asked her.

'I don't know dad. He just called me and asked me to come to his office this evening along with you and mom,' Naina said, not wishing to disclose that I wanted to inform them about Daljeet.

'I think he needs to discuss the fee part. Whatever he'll charge, we'll pay him,' Naina's mother interfered.

'No, it's not about his fees. He clarified it. Must be something else…' Naina said.

'Nonetheless, we'll go to him today. Let's see what he has to say now,' Naina's father said as he picked up the newspaper and went to the veranda to read it.

'What's the matter *didi*? Any issues?' Nisha whispered in Naina's ears.

'I don't know Nisha. In the last hearing, I told the judge whatever the truth was. Still he needs a witness to all that which Aakash isn't able to produce. I wonder what new thing has come up now...'

'Whatever… I don't care. I only know that my *didi* deserves a much better life than all this. And one day you'll get to live the life of your dreams. That's my belief *didi*,' Nisha said as she hugged Naina.

That evening in my office…

I and Kabir prepared ourselves to disclose all the facts related to Daljeet and his past to Naina and her family. We decided to do it the same day as we didn't want to waste a single minute. We had already decided to make this case as watertight as possible but without leaving any space for miscommunication. It could possibly be a mystifying scene for an outsider to see us, two opponent lawyers working for the same client and for the same cause! But sometimes you have to take a zigzag way to walk all straight, as they say.

Naina arrived at my office at 6:15 PM. She was accompanied by her parents and Nisha. As soon as they reached, my receptionist told them to come to my cabin directly. They followed suit. The moment they entered my cabin, what they saw took them to frissons. They saw me sitting with their opponent lawyer, Kabir! They looked at each other in disbelief. Naina kept looking at me with a blank expression. We realized that it would be better to ward all the misconceptions of collusion off their minds ASAP.

'Hello uncle, hello aunty,' I greeted them. Kabir preferred to remain quiet at that moment.

'Hello Aakash,' they greeted in unison.

'Please take your seat,' I said.

'Yes Aakash, tell me. Naina said you wanted to meet us,' Naina's father came directly to the point and sat bang opposite to me.

'Just a minute uncle,' I said as I called my office boy over the intercom.

'Get six cups of masala tea and two packets of ginger cookies. Quick!' I said to him.

'Naina, Nisha, please be seated. Make yourself comfortable,' I said as I realized that they hadn't yet taken their seats. They then chose the sofa kept near the window to sit.

'He is Advocate Kabir Dogra,' I introduced them to Kabir as he gave a pleasant smile to all of them. But no one reciprocated.

'Uncle, I think you have some different thoughts in mind about my calling you all here, isn't it?' I said.

'No young man, it's the same old story. Two opponent lawyers being hand in glove with each other and coaxing the litigant and his family to keep pushing on so that the case could go on and on, yeah?' Naina's father said what he understood. It wasn't his fault; a common man just cannot stand two rival lawyers working for a common cause.

I looked at Kabir and smiled. 'May I say something, uncle?' he interfered.

'No, you can't. This is not your court; it's my lawyer's office.

I don't understand, what are *you* doing here? And anyways, you have already said enough in the court. So will you kindly excuse us and leave so that we can discuss the case at our end?' Naina's father retorted hard on Kabir as anticipated by him. But he kept his cool and signaled me talk.

Meanwhile the office boy came with a big tray in his hands containing the tea cups. He kept all the cups carefully on the table before each of us, and the tray of cookies in the center of the table and went.

'What is it Aakash? You didn't tell why you called us here…' Naina's mother asked me. Naina and Nisha looked at me with a hopeful expression.

Clearing my throat, I went on to explain to them, 'Uncle, first of all, remove any apprehensions from your mind about Kabir's presence over here. We are no friends for benefits; we are here for a cause. To remove Naina from her marital mess and give justice to her. The story dates back to Naina's last hearing wherein inspite of telling the truth, the court wanted at least one evidence. I and Kabir know each other from our college days, hence I called him to my office to make him realize that he was supporting wrong people. That was the day when we both decided to dig out all the stuff related to Daljeet Singh's past and present.'

Naina's father kept looking at me with a blank expression. I couldn't gauge whether he believed in me or not; I just had to inform him about his son-in-law's misconducts till date which led to unnecessary victimisation of his daughter.

'Go on, I'm listening,' Naina's father said with frowned eyebrows.

'So uncle, finally we both decided to find out the truth, and for that we consulted a detective who extracted out all the past information about Daljeet. You will be shocked to know who he is and what all he has done till date,' I said as I pointed towards the confidential report file kept on the table. Naina and Nisha craned their necks to see the file.

'What exactly do you want to say Aakash?' Naina's mother asked me as she took her first sip.

'You will be shocked to know that Daljeet was married

before he got married to Naina,' I declared in one breath.

'What?' Naina's father howled as he got up from his chair. Naina's mother couldn't believe her ears. She kept staring at me.

'What the hell are you saying Aakash? Who has prepared this erroneous report? Are you trying to win this case using this fabricated report?' Naina's father said as he pointed towards the report file.

'May I now say something?' Kabir intervened.

'What?' Naina's father asked him in an irritated tone.

'Firstly, please understand that there's no nexus between me and Aakash, uncle. We are here to solely give justice to your daughter. And we will give her, come what may. Secondly, to fight any case, we lawyers have to know the alpha and omega of our client and our opponent too. And that's exactly what we did. We hired a private detective who discreetly pulled out all the past details of Daljeet. Let me tell you that he is an extremely inhuman person with no good virtues. I, being his lawyer, was never worried about his character and all that. He came to me with a case and I had to free him. That's it. But it is Aakash who made me realize that I was supporting a wrong person, and that could have denied justice to Naina which is her fundamental right. That was when we decided to work together,' Kabir said as he took the first sip of his tea which had turned slightly cold by then.

'How genuine is the fact that Daljeet was married before he got married to my daughter?' Naina's mother asked Kabir.

'Detective Prakash Rajput and his team have made the investigations and prepared this report. It is hundred percent accurate aunty. Let me tell you the history of Daljeet,' Kabir said as he handed the file to Naina's mother, 'Daljeet was married to one Simran in 2007. Simran was his brother's wife's foster sister. I mean, Lovleen's parents had adopted her when she was small. Daljeet did the same thing with her what he did with Naina – harassment to bring more money from her parents. He used to beat her mercilessly, much to the amusement of Lovleen who anyways hated her. One day Simran succumbed to Daljeet's atrocities and hung herself by the ceiling fan when she was alone at home.'

A wave of horror whizzed past Naina's parents. They

couldn't utter a single word. I stole a glance at Naina. She just kept staring at the floor. Naina's mother immediately kept the file on the table.

'What after that?' Naina's father asked Kabir in a sunken tone.

'Daljeet had an auto garage in Sion once upon a time. But he didn't pay attention on his business and subsequently had to shut it down as all his mechanics had left. Now he wants to open a franchise of 3N Car Care and that's why he demanded twelve lakhs from you,' Kabir said.

Eerie silence instantly filled my cabin. Nisha held Naina by her shoulders to comfort her.

I broke the silence in a few moments, 'Most important thing uncle – Daljeet is a sterile man. He cannot bear a child.'

My words gave a final, sharp blow to Naina and her family. Naina's parents kept staring at me. They were too baffled to speak anything further. Naina broke into tears and started weeping inconsolably. In an attempt to console her sister, Nisha too broke into tears. This was a situation I had never dealt with in my entire career. I had attended to scores of clients and cases, but tears and weeping was something which had never happened in my office.

Kabir came near Naina's father and held his hand and said, 'If only you would have made a background check on Daljeet before marrying your daughter to him…'

'Yes, I agree,' came Naina's father's response.

'Daljeet and his family were aware of his sterility well before he got married to Naina. But they hid this information from you all. They are a harried bunch of people uncle, but we have found a way to teach them a lesson,' I said.

Naina's father looked at me which prompted me to speak further. 'Uncle, in the court I shall continue to be your lawyer. Kabir shall be my opponent lawyer as what the protocol is. I will keep the facts from the confidential report before the judge as a proof against Daljeet. Kabir will slowly fade his arguments; he'll baselessly argue at times. Slowly but steadily, we shall drift the case in Naina's favour. This entire process will have to be as precise as clockwork, but I'm sure we'll crack it.'

'Yes uncle, that's the game plan we're going to follow,' Kabir added.

'Kabir *beta*, I am sorry that I doubted your presence over here. It isn't my fault; the way you safeguarded Daljeet in the court... I mean... we thought that you guys were upto some conventional game or something,' Naina's father said to Kabir.

'It's perfectly alright uncle, please don't apologise. Had it not been for Aakash, this case would have gone forever without any tangible judgment. But now the confidential report has ironed out most of the things. Our actual role in defending Naina starts from here,' Kabir said.

Finishing my tea, I stood up and said, 'So people, now let's come to the point. Everybody listen to me very carefully. In the next hearing, I will again ask Naina to repeat what all she has gone through. Naina, you have to blatantly answer to all my questions without hiding anything. Initially, I will plead to the court to pass the judgment based solely on your statements. Kabir will unnecessarily argue with me in this. He will raise stupid objections, most of which will be overruled by the judge. My next step will be the submission of detective Rajput's confidential report to the judge. It is often acceptable in the courts as an admissible evidence, his agency being an ISO certified organization. Kabir will again raise his doubts over the genuineness of this report. This way, Kabir will gradually decrease his own credibility in the court and disbalance the scale. In a matter of two to three hearings, the judge will pass his judgment in Naina's favour.'

Naina and his parents kept looking at me as if I was narrating a story of a movie to them. I waited for their reaction.

'But will this trick work in the court Aakash? The judge needs a concrete evidence here,' Naina's mother said.

'Like I said earlier, Detective Prakash Rajput's confidential reports are hundred percent accurate and often accepted as admissible evidence in the court, aunty. The sources from which they gather the past and current information of their subjects are genuine,' I said.

Kabir instantly got up and asked Naina, 'Naina, you said that there was a servant named Hariram who worked at Khuranas' place, right?'

The mere mention of Hariram's name sent shivers down Naina's spine. It's an amazing quality of human brain to relate people with events at times. 'Yes,' she answered.

'And you also said that he was the one who had listened to your screams that night. Am I right?' Kabir asked her.

'Yes, he did. But Harjot sent him back from the door itself. He didn't allow him to even enter my room,' Naina replied.

Then turning towards me, Kabir said, 'Aakash, detective Rajput's report says that a servant named Hariram used to work with the Khuranas until recently. He isn't heard of after that incident. Don't you think that after that night, they must have fired him, for he was the only witness of that incident?'

Kabir's question was like a dim light at the other end of the tunnel. All we had with us was the confidential report, nothing else.

'Naina, do you have any idea about his family?' I asked Naina.

'Hariram is married. He has one daughter who stays with his wife at Nashik,' Naina replied.

'Maybe they must have sent him back to Nashik after that night so that there would be no witness left,' Kabir threw a random guess.

'Yeah, possible. If only we can catch hold of him...' I ideated.

'One moment... I think his family lives somewhere in Panchvati area in Nashik...' Naina stretched her memory.

'But where in Panchvati, Naina? It's a huge area... think... he must have told you the exact location...' I helped Naina recollect Hariram's address.

'Shri Ram... Shri Ram Nagar... yes... Shri Ram Nagar in Panchvati,' Naina said.

I and Kabir looked at each other. We both knew our next step.

'We shall find him. If he has gone back to his family, I promise to produce him in the court during the subsequent hearings,' I assured Naina's parents.

'I have no words to thank you, boys. I have never seen any lawyer working so methodically. Aakash, Kabir, my blessings are with you both. Victory shall kiss your feet in this case, I'm sure. Just proceed steadily,' Naina's father said as he got up to leave. Everyone else followed suit.

'Thank you uncle. As and how this case proceeds, we will keep you informed,' I said as they left.

***

A couple of days later, I and Kabir went to Panchvati, Nashik in search of Hariram, the prime witness in Naina's case. Locating Shri Ram Nagar in Panchvati wasn't a tough job for us.

'Hariram Naik?' I asked a paan shop owner. They provide directions more accurate than Google maps in our country!

'Go straight, then take the second left. Third house on the right side,' he said, applying some lime paste on a betel leaf.

'Thank you,' I said as we hurriedly proceeded towards Hariram's house. We didn't want to make any error in tracing him.

The moment we neared his house, we spotted a small girl playing hopscotch outside. We realized that she must be his daughter.

'*Beta*, is your daddy inside?' I asked her. She kept looking at both of us as if we were aliens from Mars, then scurried inside the next moment.

A forty-ish man came out, wearing an over-broad pyjama and a kurta. 'Yes? What do you want?' he said.

'We have come from Mumbai. Are you Hariram Naik?' Kabir asked him.

'Yes, I am.'

'Hariram, we are Naina Khurana's friends. She has sent us to you,' I said.

'Naina *didi*? How is she? Is everything OK?' he asked.

'Can we come in?' I asked.

'Sure, please come in,' he said.

Hariram's was a typical chawl-system house found in most rural and suburban parts of India. These are usually joint houses with one wall common for two adjacent houses. It had an age-old asbestos roof which was sure to leak heavily in monsoons. The concrete of the walls inside was missing from many places, exposing the bricks within. There was only one room which served as a living room cum dining room cum bedroom. It made its way to a small kitchen inside with apparently no ventilation. The kitchen housed a tiny platform and a tinier bathroom with no door, just an old, torn curtain.

'Wait a minute *sahab*,' Hariram said as he hurriedly went outside. He returned with three old, over-repaired plastic chairs for us to sit. Must have borrowed them from his neighbor. Whatever.

'Please sit, *sahab*,' he said as he placed three chairs in a triangular pattern.

'Hariram, we are lawyers from Mumbai, fighting a case of dowry harassment and cheating. We need your help in it,' Kabir initiated the conversation.

'What can I do for you?' Hariram asked him.

'Nothing much. Just tell us entirely what happened that night with Naina,' I said.

'Which night? Oh, you mean *that* night? Nothing *sahab*, Naina *didi* wasn't feeling well. She had a stomach ache,' Hariram said.

'Stomach ache? Who told you? Tell us everything Hariram,' I said.

'Harjot *bhaiya* told me. That night I heard Naina *didi's* screams. Must be one thirty or two. When I knocked her door, Harjot *bhaiya* opened it and informed me that she had a stomach pain. Harjot *bhaiya's* presence in Naina *didi's* room was a baffling scene in itself. I smelt a rat, but couldn't do anything *sahab*. After that I heard Naina *didi's* screams intermittently. I realized it was much more than just a stomach ache. But there was nothing I could have done *sahab*. A while later I saw Harjot *bhaiya* and Daljeet *bhaiya* dragging Naina *didi* out of the house. She was in an unconscious state. This strengthened my doubt further. They must have thought that I was fast asleep and didn't see them, but I saw them clearly. Next morning, Daljeet *bhaiya* called me and all of a sudden told me to leave their house forever as they no longer needed me. Since then, I am here with my family. I now work for a local wine shop as their godown supervisor,' Hariram said.

'Now I understand the whole game,' Kabir said, 'OK Hariram, if I ask you to come to Mumbai and tell this in front of the judge, will you do it?'

'Judge?!' a befuddled Hariram asked.

'Dear Hariram, this is not as simple as it seems to you. They raped Naina that night. Both of them. When she fell unconscious, they just threw her in the hospital. Fearing your presence there, you being the prime witness, Daljeet fired you for no apparent reason,' I clarified.

'What?' Hariram said as he stood up, 'What are you saying *sahab*? Where is Naina *didi*? How is she now?'

'She survived all this Hariram, please sit. She's now staying with her parents. Her case has gone to the court and I am her lawyer,' I said, all too quick for him to register.

'My God! I don't believe this! Had I known the truth, I would have complained to the police the very next day,' Hariram said.

'Good you didn't. Had Daljeet or Harjot known that you saw them taking Naina outside, or worse, you complained to the police, they would have harmed you and even your family Hariram,' Kabir said.

'What needs to be done now?' he asked.

'We are preparing her case. We just want you to come to the court and speak the truth before the judge. Rest, we'll manage,' I said.

'Sure, *sahab*. For Naina *didi*, I'll surely do that. I only hope she forgets all this and starts her life afresh. She has already faced a lot of trauma in this house. I've seen that,' Hariram said as we got up to leave.

'Thank you for your cooperation Hariram,' I said as we left.

In the next few days, I and Kabir collated all the requisite information on papers as per the court etiquette to strengthen Naina's case. We decided to register the case directly with Mumbai High Court. I took a date from the court and sent a legal notice to Daljeet to appear before the court. In a fit of rage, Daljeet did something which was totally unexpected by me or Kabir.

12

'Fifty ledger papers, ten stamp papers of hundred rupees each and twenty revenue stamps.' I ordered my usual stuff over the phone. The stamp paper vendor had always been generous enough to deliver things at my office.

Naina's case paper file was almost ready. All the statements, proofs, dates and events and most importantly, facts and figures from detective Rajput's confidential report were well incorporated in her papers. With our strategy set for the subsequent hearings, there was hardly any room for dismissal of justice to Naina.

Just then, my phone buzzed. It was an unknown number of a landline with the STD code of Mumbai, 022. I answered it after two rings.

'Hello?'

'Aakash Khanna?' an untamed, irritable man at the other end spoke.

'Who's this?' I asked, still busy with my paperwork.

'Bilal Ilyaasi. Leave Naina's case.'

'What? Who's speaking?' I said as I stopped my work. It is not every day that lawyers get such calls to leave their cases.

'I said I am Bilal Ilyaasi. Leave Naina's case, else you will be in trouble,' he said.

'Where are you calling from? And who has asked you to call me and tell this crap?' I said as I quickly tapped on the *call record* button of my phone.

'Don't ask stupid questions, lawyer. Leave them for your court hearings. Do whatever, but don't involve yourself in Naina Khurana's case. Otherwise your parents will repent on their decision of making you a lawyer.'

'What the… listen… hello… hello…' I said, but only heard a click in response. I quickly dialed that number back but no one answered it. Then I called up Kabir. I had to inform him.

'Do one thing, text the number to Prakash. He'll find out

its exact location,' he suggested. I called up Prakash and gave him the call details. He took the number from me and called back with its exact location in twenty minutes flat.

'Kabir, the call was from a general merchant's landline in Sai market, Worli village. It's a PCO number,' I again called Kabir and informed him.

'It's clear Aakash – Daljeet must have hired somebody to call and threaten you. I think now he is afraid as you have sent him a notice regarding the next hearing. Good that he is, his fear alone will ease things for us,' Kabir said.

'That's true. But this won't be sufficient to trace the caller Kabir. It is an ordinary PCO number. No use complaining to police as well,' I said.

'That's right. But don't worry, I don't think he'll call again. But if he does, do inform immediately,' Kabir said.

'Sure, I will.'

After two days…

I was about to leave for Sessions Court for the hearing of one of my regular cases when my phone buzzed of an incoming call. It was again a landline number, but this time a different one as I had saved the number from which Bilal had called me. I answered it in just one ring as I was getting late.

'Hello…'

'Aakash Khanna?' I heard the same voice again.

'Bilal Ilyaasi… tell me,' I said, rather teased.

'I guess you are out of Naina Khurana's case now,' he said.

'No. Your guess is totally wrong,' I replied.

'Look boss, don't take me or my calls lightly. We may be smooth on telephone, but rough in person. You may have to regret later for not having abided by what I'm telling you.'

'Firstly, you coward, stop blowing your own trumpet. Secondly, call me from your direct number instead of changing PCOs every time. And thirdly, stay out of others' affairs. If you don't have any work, search for one. But stop peeping in others' lives,' I snapped back.

'I am warning you for the last time Aakash, leave Naina

Khurana's case. It will be better for you,' Bilal said.

'Who the hell you think you are? And how dare you talk like this with a lawyer? We are made to take cases. We are made to give justice to our clients. What the hell has all this to do with you? You better mind your own business now and don't dare to call back,' I retorted with thrice my volume.

Startled with the loud telephonic conversation in my cabin, my receptionist rushed in. 'Any problem Aakash Sir?' she asked. I just shook my head and signaled her to go back. She left.

'Listen you son of a bitch, don't think that as you wear a black coat, you can do whatever you want. There are things beyond your fucking law and order. And who cares about law in this country? Here only we decide. We are that part of the society where even your courts and laws come to knees. And mind you, we act fast. At least faster than your court decisions. So abide by what I'm saying. It'll be better for you. Else one day you'll wake up only to find that both your limbs are missing,' Bilal said.

'You bastard! What do you think of yourself? You'll abuse me, ridicule the law and order machinery here and I'll be afraid? Fucking asshole, stay out of all this. And whosoever has hired you to do all this crap, tell him that no such tricks are going to work now. Keep the phone and don't dare to call back again,' I screamed. He disconnected the call.

Within moments, my entire face was in sweat. Sometimes certain conversations overshoot the cooling capacity of air conditioners! I wiped my face, took my belongings and stormed out of my cabin.

That evening I met Kabir at his office and gave him my conversation details with Bilal.

'Don't take his call lightly, but don't be afraid either,' Kabir said.

'Yeah… but how to put an end to his calls man? He has called me twice. He changes PCO every time. It's difficult to even trace him or get him arrested. I don't think complaining to police will help,' I said.

'No no, don't involve the police. We are already floating a strategy to save Naina; nothing should come even closer to it. Not even police,' Kabir said.

'I gave him a good peace of mind in the morning. Maybe he won't call again. But can't say anything,' I pondered.

'Max to max, he'll call again and threaten you. If things go out of control, just seek police protection till the next hearing. In any case, we're going to crack Naina's case in a hearing or two,' Kabir suggested. His words made sense to me.

Next day
Around 11:30 AM…

'But Sir… my image is at stake. I am an upcoming model, as you know. Now she threatens to defame me in the court by alleging that I'm a gay!' Vicky Saldhana, one of my clients, said. He was a tad above six feet and had chiseled biceps and broad shoulders. He claimed to spend four hours in his gym every day. He had married his three-year old girlfriend some time back, but both headed for a divorce within six months of marriage. He referred to the failure of his marriage as just a *compatibility issue*. For youngsters today, marriage is just like buying a new smartphone – they're never satisfied with the features of their existing model!

'That I expected Vicky. Most girls nowadays are resorting to such stupid allegations. Let her say what she wants to. Our job is to collect as many witnesses as we can. Firstly, we'll have to pull her call details of last three months,' I said as I heard some commotion outside my chamber.

Before I could go out to check on it, five masked men kicked open the door of my cabin and stormed inside. Their masks just exposed their eyes and nostrils, nothing else. The one standing in front asked me, 'Are you advocate Aakash?' while rest of the others were his sidekicks and scanned my entire cabin.

That was a familiar voice for me. 'Who are you? And how come you storm in my cabin without my permission?' I said.

'I am going to do a lot of things without your permission now,' he said as one of his men hit the glass door of my showcase with his iron rod. It was splintered the very next moment to small, shapeless bits.

'What do you want? Who are you?' I asked him, this time in a milder tone. It was useless to show my bravado, given that they were five men brandishing iron rods in their hands. One of them even had a country made revolver tucked in his trousers which was easily visible.

'I want you to listen to me... to abide by what I say. I tried that over the phone, but it seems you needed this treatment badly...' the one in front said as I interrupted him.

'Bilal Ilyaasi?' I asked him, startled.

'Yes advocate, I am Bilal,' he said as he came closer to me, 'What were you saying that day over the phone? Say again.'

'Look Bilal, I don't have time to discuss all this. Please move out of my office. You cannot threaten and let me do things as per your wish. Law has certain protocols and it's our duty to follow them. But if you –' I said as he interrupted me.

'Protocols, my ass! I know very well what happens in a court and how fast your courts work. Leave all that crap aside. Come on, give me all the files and papers related to Naina Khurana's case,' Bilal rebuked.

Fortunately, I had kept Naina's case file at Kabir's office the previous evening. Had it not been for it, I would have to wash my hands off that file.

'It's not yet ready. I've given it to one of the senior lawyers to scrutinize its contents,' I lied. This all the more enraged Bilal.

'Break his bones. All of them. Ansari, you manage outside,' he screamed at his men and moved aside. Before things could proceed further, the chisel bodied, biceped and broad shouldered Vicky Saldhana got up and ran away like a rat!

Three men came forward and started hitting me. They punched me on my belly, one after the other. Two men begin to ransack my office. They threw all the papers, files and stationeries on the floor. Ansari, who was asked to go outside, bolted the main door of my office from inside and threatened my receptionist to keep mum. Bilal's men continued to hit me wherever and however they could. I was punched nearly six times right on my lips by one of them. I started bleeding profusely and told them to stop. But instead, Bilal took an iron rod from one of his men, came forward and hit on my right leg, just below the knee. I screamed at the top of my voice for I couldn't bear the pain. Then bending on his knees, Bilal held my head by my hair and said, 'Final warning, don't go soft on me. Leave Naina Khurana's case. Handover her file to us. I'll send my man in the evening to collect it. Any more refusals and I'll kill you. Understand?'

I wasn't in a position to reply even a customary yes or no as by then both my lips were swollen. But I wanted to reply to him. I just raised my right hand and somehow managed to show him my middle finger. Before he and his men could react, I went unconscious and fell on the floor.

'Keep an eye on him,' Bilal said to one of his men as they hurriedly exited my office. The moment they were out of sight, my receptionist called up Kabir and informed him everything. In no time, he rushed to my office and saw me lying on the floor. It wasn't difficult for him to realize who was behind all this. He immediately called for an ambulance and took me to hospital. My condition worsened with time.

'Slight internal bleeding in the intestine. We have given two injections to control it. There are two deep cuts on the left jaw which we have stitched. Right leg has a hairline fracture. We'll have to keep him in ICU for the next forty eight hours under observation,' the attending doctor said to Kabir who was waiting outside my room.

'When can I meet him doctor?' Kabir asked.

'Anytime after he regains his senses,' the doctor said.

I came in my senses at around eight at night. The hospital ceiling and the characteristic smell of medicines made me all the more uncomfortable. I slowly scanned the whole room only to discover that it was a hospital ICU! Just then, a nurse who was passing by saw me and immediately rushed to call the doctor.

'Good evening Mr. Aakash! How are you feeling now?' the doctor asked me with a pleasant smile.

'Painful!' is what I could just answer him.

'It will remain for some time. We have been timely administering injections to you through your saline. Don't worry, you will be fine in a few days,' he said.

I nodded and attempted to give him a smile, but I couldn't. The edges of my lips were too swollen to even smile.

'Now you take rest. And don't think too much. You'll be discharged in a few days. I'll send your friend in. He's waiting outside since afternoon,' the doctor said as he left.

'You may go in to meet him. But remember, not more than ten minutes. It's ICU,' the doctor said to Kabir.

'Sure. When will he be shifted in the private ward?' Kabir asked him.

'Looks like in the next three days,' the doctor said.

'OK. Thank you doctor,' Kabir said as he rushed to the ICU to see me.

My ICU had twelve beds, all equipped with everything that a dying patient needs by his side. Three patients were kept on dialysis, one of them being a five year-old girl. There was an accident case of a twentysome guy. Surgeons had to implant Titanium rods in both of his legs. The patient by my left side had a severe heart attack. His heart rate was being continually monitored on the screen. Every thirty minutes a nurse would come and take his readings to show to his attending cardiologist.

Kabir came and stood near me with a blank expression. He couldn't utter a word on seeing my condition.

'Relax dude, I'm still alive,' I said, uttering each word slowly. He smiled.

'So sorry for all this *yaar*. But never mind, you'll be out of ICU in the next three to four days,' Kabir said.

'Sit *na*,' I said, pointing to a small stainless steel stool kept aside. Kabir shifted it near my bed and sat on it.

'Listen,' Kabir said, 'who were they?'

'Bilal Ilyaasi and his men. He wanted Naina's case file but I told him that I had given it to my senior to check it,' I said.

'Aakash! You could have called me… I could have come there and given it to them. At least they wouldn't have done this to you…' Kabir said.

'This is nothing if compared to the trauma what Naina has faced with Daljeet. And we have sworn to liberate her from all that, haven't we?' I said.

'Yeah, that's true. But anything could have happened to you today,' Kabir said.

'So what? I would have become a martyr then, what else?' I winked. At least it lightened the moment.

'Shut up man! Ok listen, the doctor has told me not to stay here for more than ten minutes. I'll wait in the waiting lobby on third floor. You rest. And don't think too much now,' Kabir said and left.

Soon, a male nurse brought my dinner. Steamed rice... dal thinner than water... two chapatis and boiled, tasteless potato *subji*! The food just refused to go in. But I had to have it as I was being given a lot of medicines and injections. That night I thought a lot about Naina.

Where did she go wrong? An ideal daughter... an ideal wife... an ideal daughter-in-law... what else does one expect out of a girl? She excelled in everything but God had different plans for her journey. Naina had an option to marry the person who loved her a lot. Me. But she didn't exercise it; instead she proceeded with a totally unknown person and gave the reins of her life in his bare hands. And he played with her life as miserably as he could. So much so that he even allowed his brother to have sex with her in an inebriated state. In the midst of all this, did anyone think how Naina must have felt while going through all this? She could have ended up her life; many girls do that. But Naina wanted her life back. She wanted what she desired and fought for what she deserved.

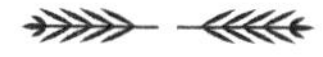

13

Next day…

'But how did all this happen?' Naina asked Kabir. He called her up to inform about my condition.

'He was getting threatening calls from one Bilal Ilyaasi to leave your case since a few days, but he took them lightly. He didn't anticipate that they'd actually come to his office. Anyways, find some time and come to Jairaj hospital whenever you can,' Kabir said.

'Threatening calls to leave my case? That means Daljeet is there behind all this… Anyways, I am coming to hospital as soon as I can,' Naina said and hung up. She called Payal and Aarti and informed them about my condition, soon after which the trio reached my hospital to see me.

'Good morning Mr. Aakash! How are you feeling now? Has the pain reduced?' the attending doctor asked me. He had come to check on me and record my body readings.

'Hello Sir! Pretty much better now. But I feel the taste of medicines in my mouth all the time,' I complained.

'That'll remain for some days, don't worry,' he said as the nurse next to him checked on the medicines, salines and injections and replaced the old bottles and vials with new ones.

By around 10:00 AM, Naina reached the hospital along with Aarti and Payal. Aarti enquired for me with the receptionist, 'Excuse me! Which is Aakash Khanna's ward?'

The receptionist gave a quick glance on her computer and said, 'ICU. Fifth floor ma'am.' The girls hurriedly took the elevator and reached my floor.

'How is he now?' Naina asked Kabir. He was still waiting outside my room.

'Better. Much better now,' Kabir said.

'Can we see him?' Payal asked Kabir.

'Yes. The meeting timings for ICU patients are from ten to

eleven. I just met him. You guys can go in, but don't make noise. Listen, I am going home. Need to freshen up for the day. I am here since yesterday morning. Will be back in an hour,' Kabir said.

'Okay, we are here only,' Payal said as the girls entered my ICU. They glanced every patient one by one till Aarti spotted me, 'There he is!'

'Shhh! Quiet!' Payal warned her as they walked towards me.

The moment Naina saw me, she started weeping. I was too helpless to get up and console her. She wept and wept inconsolably.

'Naina! Stop weeping sweety. He'll be okay...' Aarti consoled her.

'What is all this Aakash?' Payal asked me.

'Just like that! Felt like having a picnic in a hospital ICU...' I joked to bring Naina back in mood. I didn't want anyone to feel my pain.

'Shut up Aakash! Who were they?' Aarti asked me.

I went quiet. I didn't want to reveal the details to her, but couldn't even avoid a straight, face-on question by her.

'Your silence speaks a million words Aakash. Sorry for all this *yaar*,' Payal said.

'It's okay. I'm in a profession to safeguard law, aren't I? So there are chances that I may encounter people who don't like to stay in the limits of law. In turn, they won't even like me. Happens...' I winked.

'It's all because of me. Aakash, please leave my case. I cannot let this happen to you,' Naina said.

'Don't be silly Naina. This has nothing to do with you. And secondly, a local goon tells me to stop working on a case and I'll abide by him! That's what you think about me?' I said.

Wiping her tears with her kerchief, Naina said, 'Aakash, I'm withdrawing my case. I have no rights to let this happen to you. Today they just injured you. Tomorrow they'll –'

'They'll what Naina?' I interrupted her, 'People of this stratum of society think that they'll play around with the law and law protectors and get away free? No Naina, this isn't what we have studied in our law manuals. They should be punished. And they *will be* punished. Don't even think of withdrawing your case.'

'So what do I do? Keep on letting this happen with you? No, I can't,' Naina said in a higher tone.

'Speak slowly madam, this is ICU,' a nurse attending a patient two beds away from me said to Naina.

'Whatever, but I and Kabir have vowed to remove you from the tangled mess you are in. We'll do whatever it takes us to do. But you be firm in your statements in the court. All I want is truth to come out of you, nothing else,' I said.

'But Aakash, what if such thing happens with you or Kabir again?' Payal asked.

'That I can't promise. But one thing I can assure you – I'll liberate your friend. She deserves a happier and content life,' I said, looking at Naina.

'Ask for police protection till the case gets completed *na*,' Aarti ideated.

'It doesn't happen that way Aarti. Max to max, a constable will be posted outside my office and home for a week. Will he be able to handle four armed goons? Tell me?' I said.

The girls went quiet. They couldn't argue further. 'Listen girls, you are thinking too much. Don't worry about me. I'll be out of here in a week. Just think that I met with a small accident and am admitted here,' I said to alleviate their mood.

'How did you find the hospital food?' Naina asked me.

'Lip smacking! I've recommended the cook here to apply in Marriot,' I joked.

Naina smiled. The last I saw her smile was during our college days.

'Don't eat here. I'll bring food for you from today. Take care,' Naina whispered, but loud enough for Aarti and Payal to hear. They smiled at each other.

'Cheers girls! Come again to bore me,' I said as they bid good bye and left.

***

Kabir cancelled all his appointments for the day and came

back to hospital at around twelve noon. 'Have the girls left?' he asked me.

'Yeah, long back,' I said.

'We'll have to request the court to shift the hearing at a later date till you recover fully,' Kabir said.

'Just let me be on my toes back, Kabir. I'll teach the Khuranas a lesson they'll never forget. Bilal is just a hired goon. He has nothing to do with me or Naina's case. He just did what he was told to do. But Daljeet…? You know what… today I saw Naina smile for the first time since our college days. Doesn't she represent a victim of harassment, cheating and abuse? She did what was expected out of her. And look at the life she's leading today. No Kabir no, I won't spare that Daljeet. I won't spare him,' I said.

'Ok, whatever. But first you be alright. Don't think about the case as of now. Just make sure you eat and rest properly. Let the medicines and treatment work on you. Only then you'll be able to fight in the court, isn't it?' Kabir said.

I looked at him and gave him a mild fist-to-fist punch.

***

I was shifted to a private, air conditioned ward after three days. My attending doctor asked me to take complete bed rest for the next seven to ten days.

'Why did you take so much trouble Naina? I told you *na*, I get Marriot – quality food here,' I said to Naina. She had brought mildly spiced *aloo parathas* with chilly – coriander chutney and curd for me for dinner.

'Keep quiet and eat your food,' she said as she carefully opened the silver foil containing the *parathas*.

'Mmmmmm…. Heaven!' I exclaimed as I took my first bite. I was allowed to eat only homemade food if I didn't opt for the hospital food.

'Have it with curd,' she said as she opened a small stainless steel container containing curd.

I gulped the food like a street beggar who was given some food after many days. She kept looking at me but didn't say anything.

'Superb!' I said as I finished all my four parathas and belched.

'I'll bring lunch and dinner daily for you,' Naina said as she packed all the containers and stuffed them back in her bag.

'It's really not an issue having food here. I can manage Naina,' I said.

'You are risking your life so that I can have a better tomorrow. Can't I do this much for you Aakash?' Naina asked me, looking right inside my eyes.

We kept looking at each other for a few moments. 'Meeting time over,' the on-duty nurse came to us and said.

Naina lowered her eyes, quickly zipped her hand bag and got up to leave.

'I like *gobhi parathas* too. Feel like having them tomorrow for lunch,' I said. Naina just nodded and said, 'Good night Aakash,' as she left.

Did something just click? What did she think when our eyes met? Why in the first place did she bring food for me? Why did she lock her eyes with me? The girl whom I immensely loved once upon a time brought food for me so that I don't have to eat the bland hospital food. But why did she have to think of this? Will she come tomorrow? I dosed off at one, pondering over Naina and the time we spent together during our college days.

Days went by and my condition improved. I could stand on my feet, walk short distances and even slowly climb the stairs. On the other end, Kabir fine tuned the case, thus eliminating any room for errors. He updated me on the nuances of Naina's case every evening. I diligently took my medicines and responded to my treatment very well. Naina gave me home made food twice a day which additionally quickened my recovery. She would patiently sit near me and wait for me to finish my food. Something had kindled between us, though we didn't say anything to each other. All what kept coming in my mind was – *She's a conservative girl. She's still married. Don't say anything to her. Keep mum, at least till her case is finished.*

However, I decided to share this with Kabir.

'We have got the date of our next hearing. It's on the third of May. Mumbai High Court,' Kabir said. He had come to my ward to discuss the finer points on Naina's case, our every evening ritual.

'Okay. Just to top it up Kabir, convey this date to Hariram. He should be present in the court for all the hearings of this case,' I said.

'I called him this afternoon and told him to be present in the court on the third of May and also for the subsequent hearings. He said he'll surely come,' Kabir said.

'Make sure you have the soft copy of detective Prakash's confidential report in your system. We have to preserve it till the case gets completed,' I added.

'Yup. I have it.'

'Kabir... *yaar* I want to tell you something,' I said.

'What happened? You fell for a nurse or something?' Kabir winked.

'Not nurse, someone else,' I said.

'*Acha*! Whom?'

I collected all my guts and said, 'Naina.'

'What? Are you out of your mind Aakash?' Kabir bawled. Fortunately, we were in my private ward.

'Listen Kabir... don't misunderstand me or my feelings for her. I –' I said as Kabir interrupted me.

'*Are* what feelings? You sound as if you're one brick short of a full load dude! She's someone else's wife. Since four years now. I hope you didn't tell all this to her...' Kabir said.

'Kabir listen to the whole thing please...' I almost pleaded.

'What...?' he said, vexation beginning to get the better of him.

'Kabir, over these years Naina got nothing but humiliation and disdain not only from her in-laws but also from her husband. She turned down my proposal only to satiate her parents' wish. Life has again brought us face to face after so many years. Why else did she not go to some other lawyer but me? God has some plans for us, I think. She cares for me Kabir, it is visible. I can see it in her eyes. She too has a thing for me. But she won't confess it. Not over her dead body. She understands that she's married to someone, and that falling for someone else is something she won't let happen with herself, I know,' I elucidated.

Kabir listened to me with rapt attention. He went towards the window and opened the blinds. 'How can you be so sure that she too has a thing for you? Did she tell you anything?' he asked.

'No! Not at all. Neither have I. But it seems there's an X-factor between us. Ever since I've landed in this hospital, she hasn't missed out on a single day to come and see me... to give me home-cooked food... to remind me of medicines. I don't want to say that she does all this because she has fallen for me and all that. But certainly there is something unusual... like you feel when you're in...' I said.

'You are in...? What?' Kabir nudged.

'... In love Kabir,' I said. My words made a little sense to him now.

'You sure, this is love Aakash?' Kabir asked.

'Yes Kabir. This is love. I can feel it. Again. For her,' I said, 'And I'm sure she too feels the same for me.'

'Oh... kay. Let's do one thing Aakash. First let us finish her case. That's our primary work. Once she gets her divorce from that pig, put your feelings before her. Let us see what's her say in this. But as of now, let us concentrate only on her case, not on her,' Kabir said.

'Sure! Kabir... thanks *yaar*!' I said.

He smiled.

In the following days, I recuperated and eventually got discharged from the hospital. The day of the first hearing of Naina's case was just a week away. I and Kabir made sure to include all the finer points associated with this case. We had all our papers, arguments, strategy and most importantly, an eye witness ready. We prepped to the finest detail as the hearing date came nearer.

Finally, the 3rd of May arrived with ours being on the case list of Mumbai High Court.

14

First hearing of Naina Khurana v/s Daljeet Khurana case.

Mumbai High Court,
Dr. Kane Road, Fort, Mumbai.

Judge – Hon. Justice Sohrabjee Billimoria.

'Your honour, I'm the lawyer of the victim of dowry harassment, Mrs. Naina Daljeet Khurana. This case, vide chargesheet number 42313, was being handled in the Sessions Court. But I have applied it in the honourable High Court as I and my client weren't satisfied with the judgment thereof. May I open my statement?' I asked the presiding judge, Honourable Justice Sohrabjee Billimoria with a slight bow.

'Yes, you may,' he said.

Justice Sohrabjee Billimoria had an experience of thirty two years as a judge. Having served the courts of all strata of our judicial system, he was transferred from Manipur High Court and posted to Mumbai High Court six months ago. He had an unbeatable record of consuming the least number of dates of hearing for any case and punishing the guilty as early as possible. He never believed in litigants and witnesses swear by the Holy *Bhagwadgita* and never allowed anyone to do that in his court.

'Thank you my lord,' I said as I opened the case, 'Naina Daljeet Khurana was married to Daljeet Singh Khurana some four years back. Everything was okay only initially, but soon the true colours of her husband Daljeet Singh Khurana came out. He would hit her for small reasons, abuse her and her family unnecessarily and most important of all, harass her to bring money from her parents. My lord, till here this may seem like a regular family affair, but things got worse when he started demanding a huge sum from her parents through her, twelve lakhs. He wanted to start his own car servicing showroom and for that he needed a capital.

He repeatedly asked Naina to bring the money from her parents. Had it been a lakh or two, she would have thought over it. But asking for this huge a sum was out of question for her. When she repeatedly turned down his request, rather demand, Daljeet Singh Khurana raped her along with his brother Harjot Singh Khurana. The duo then dumped her to glory hospital and never came back to take her. I expect nothing but justice and only justice for my client. That's all me lord.'

All eyes were glued to Naina and her family. She wore a stern expression which spoke a million words.

'Advocate Kabir, your witness please,' the judge said.

'What a lovely speech!' Kabir said as he got up, came forward and clapped, loud enough for it to echo in the courtroom, 'My lord, it is not uncommon for women today to take the support of dowry harassment or marital rape or whatever. Whether or not they have a witness or even a reasonable backing for their allegation, they scream on the top of their voice and let everybody know what all happened with them. But the question here is, does anything even take place for which they create the whole rumpus in the society?'

'Advocate Kabir, what do you want to say? It isn't clear,' the judge said.

'My lordship, I just want to say that my client, Daljeet Singh Khurana and his family are one of the most respected and law abiding citizens of this city. Right from the beginning, my client Daljeet has a steady record. Neither he nor anybody from his family has ever been embroiled in even a controversy - rapes and dowry demands, as put forth by my capable opponent lawyer go out of question. Now coming to his wife, Naina Daljeet Khurana... well, she has a habit of blowing things out of proportion for every miniscule thing. Initially, everything seemed hunky dory to my client. But soon, Naina's true colours came to light. For instance, she'd bend her ATM card completely if she couldn't withdraw cash from an ATM. She'd argue with a taxi driver over a change of five rupees or even less than that. Once it so happened that she filled her shopping cart at Big Bazaar with the essentials for the entire month but kept the cart there itself and walked out as there were four people standing before her on the billing counter! I can give more such examples of her unruly nature to the court, but I respect the court's timings and request you to dismiss this case today itself as her statements and allegations do not hold any water. That's all me lord.'

I stole a glance at Naina and signaled her to relax; all this was a part of our strategy.

'It is very easy to throw such lines on a woman, my lord. Had it been the other way round, my capable opponent lawyer would have some other story to tell you. Whatever, I would like to call my client, Naina Daljeet Khurana in the witness box,' I said.

'Permission granted,' the judge said.

Naina got up and walked up to the witness box. Everybody craned their necks to have a look at her.

'Mrs. Naina Daljeet Khurana, by whom –' I began my questioning as Naina stopped me.

'Please, I request you to call me just Naina, not by my full name. It sulks,' she said.

'As you please. So Naina, by whom were you introduced to Daljeet for the first time?' I asked.

'My parents had fixed up my marriage.'

'Okay. So you didn't know him before marriage, I guess...' I said.

'No, I didn't,' Naina said.

'You said you've been married to him for four long years. You also said that you've been victimised for every small thing in your life, right?' I asked.

'Yes. My father had already given him enough during my marriage. But that didn't quench his thirst I guess. Now to start his business he needed money and expected it to come from my parents. When I was staid about not asking it from my father, he lost his cool. One night, he and his brother Harjot raped me and threw me in glory hospital. I may not be having any evidence or witness for this, but I am speaking the truth Sir,' Naina said to the judge.

'So weren't they arrested?' I asked.

'They were, but they walked free as they heavily bribed the

inspector who was investigating this case,' Naina said.

The judge turned to Daljeet and Harjot who were seated in the first row. He couldn't see any remorse on their faces.

'I would like to cross examine her, my lord,' Kabir intervened, as planned between us.

'Go ahead.'

'So Mrs. Naina Daljeet Khurana, I guess –' Kabir started his questioning when Naina stopped him.

'Please don't call me –' Naina said.

'OK OK… I'll call you only Naina,' Kabir interrupted her back, 'So Naina, I guess you have made up your mind to malign my client and your husband's image today, yeah?'

'One cannot malign anything which doesn't hold any value,' Naina said. Smart answer!

'Mrs. Naina, language please,' the judge interceded.

'You may not decide that. Anyways, tell me one thing Naina, if you find your husband and his family so cruel, how come you spent four years with them? Shouldn't you have walked out of your marriage long back?' Kabir asked Naina.

'I could have. And I should have. But coming from a middle-class family, such walk-outs are generally not accepted; in fact they are misjudged by the society and even by the girls' parents. If I would have done that, my parents would have convinced me to go back. It happens with every second girl as we all know,' Naina said.

'OK. In your four year – long marriage, why didn't you have any kids? Not a single one… Why?' Kabir threw his pawn. Everything was going as per our plan.

'This question may be asked to Daljeet,' Naina said.

'Daljeet? Why would I ask this to Daljeet? It's you who has to bear a child and give birth to him, right? So I should ask this to you,' a perplexed Kabir said.

'Can a wife alone bear a child? Doesn't she need her husband's cooperation in this?' Naina answered as everyone present in the courtroom burst out laughing.

'Order, order,' the judge said, 'Mrs. Naina, please stick to your replies and arguments.'

'Sorry your honour,' Naina said.

'Oh, so you mean your husband didn't cooperate with you in –' Kabir said as the judge keyed in again, 'Advocate Kabir, go easy.'

'Sure, my lord. OK Naina, I come back to my question. Why no child in your four year – old marriage?' Kabir asked.

'The problem can be from either side. I raised this concern several times before Daljeet. I requested him many times that we both undergo a fertility check for this. But every time he denied doing this, saying that the problem was from my end. I got my check up done several months ago. My results were absolutely normal. Now ask the same thing to him please,' Naina said.

'You bloody bitch!' Daljeet suddenly started abusing Naina as he heard her reply, 'You are trying to slander my image in this court? What the hell do you think of yourself? You'll say anything and the judge will listen to it?'

'Order, order. Daljeet, don't break the decorum of the court,' the judge warned him but he continued.

'Sterile whores like you have no other option but to blame others,' Daljeet howled. Had it not been a courtroom, I would have killed him that day.

'Mr Daljeet, I told you to stop. And control your language. You are sitting in the High Court,' the judge stepped in again, 'Advocate Kabir, please tell your client not to use foul language in my court.'

'You couldn't keep me happy, is that my fault? You couldn't be a good wife, is that my fault? Forget all that, you couldn't even give me a child, is that again my fault, you sterile lady?' Daljeet continued to bark.

'Advocate Kabir, if your client doesn't stop here, he'll be heavily charged for violating the court norms. Tell him to sit down and be quiet before I hold him in contempt,' the judge finally warned Kabir.

Kabir signaled Daljeet to stop howling and take his seat. A drop of tear rolled down Naina's cheek. She wiped it and composed herself.

'Sorry for my client's reaction. OK Naina, do you have

your fertility test reports with you? Kabir asked her.

'No. I misplaced them some days back.'

'Then how can the court believe that your reports were normal?' Kabir asked. I preferred not to interfere as all these questions were a part of our game plan.

'I am ready for a check up again,' a confident Naina said.

'Advocate Aakash, would you like to say anything in this?' the judge asked me.

'No, your honour. The tests may be conducted, but on both of them,' I said.

'Here I fully agree with Advocate Aakash. Let the tests be conducted. We'll come to know who's at fault for their barren marriage,' Kabir added.

'In accordance with the arguments presented by Advocate Aakash and Advocate Kabir in Naina Khurana rape case today, this court orders Naina Daljeet Khurana and her husband Daljeet Singh Khurana to undergo their fertility tests at the state – run Lokmanya Tilak hospital at Sion. It may be further noted that Advocate Aakash needs to make a further, detailed investigation in the allegation of rape by her client, Naina Daljeet Khurana against her husband Daljeet Singh Khurana. The next date for the hearing of this case is eleventh of May. This court is adjourned,' Justice Sohrabjee Billimoria announced.

15

Second hearing of Naina Khurana v/s Daljeet Khurana case.

Mumbai High Court,
Dr. Kane Road, Fort, Mumbai.

Judge – Hon. Justice Sohrabjee Billimoria.

Naina's case had become an overnight sensation for most of the people who had witnessed the court hearings of the first date. The case details spread almost like forest fire, attracting more attendees for the second hearing, so much so that even a press reporter from *Dainik Jagran* marked his presence. Everybody wanted to know who was at fault. In a way, Naina represented an endured woman of the society who was a victim of dowry harassment and marital rape. Now all what people wanted to see was the fate of this case.

The moment Justice Sohrabjee Billimoria entered the courtroom and stepped on his dais, everybody stood up. I and Kabir bowed to him, a ritual every lawyer follows.

Going through Naina's file to refresh the statements of the first hearing, the judge said, 'Please submit the fertility test reports of Naina Daljeet Khurana and Daljeet Singh Khurana.'

The stenographer handed over two sealed envelopes to the court peon, who in turn handed them over to the judge. He tore the envelopes and removed the test reports to see them. There was a pin drop silence in the courtroom; everybody wanted to know the report details.

Carefully scrutinizing both the test reports, the judge said, 'Mr Daljeet Singh Khurana, please come in the witness box.'

Daljeet got up and walked up to the witness box.

'Have you ever undergone a fertility test?' the judge asked him.

Daljeet remained silent.

The judge asked him again, 'Mr Daljeet Singh Khurana, I repeat my question once more - have you ever undergone a fertility test?'

'N… No Sir,' came out Daljeet's reply.

'Anything wrong, my lord?' Kabir intervened.

'Yes, Advocate Kabir. Naina's fertility test reports are absolutely normal while your client Daljeet's aren't. He has a normal sperm count but there's no motility in them. In a layman's language, his sperms cannot swim across and fertilize a womb,' the judge said.

Justice Sohrabjee Billimoria's words came as a rude shock to everyone present in the court. Kabir faked an impressive surprise expression that could take even a Bollywood actor to shame. Everything in the court was working in sync with our plan, and here I was not to unnecessarily blow Naina's trumpet. I chose to remain silent.

Then turning towards Daljeet, the judge asked, 'Daljeet, were you aware of this condition?'

'No Sir! Even I'm surprised to hear this. I think there is some goof – up. May I get it done again from my friend's private pathology lab?' Daljeet asked.

'Objection, my lord,' I intervened.

'Objection overruled,' the judge said, then turned towards Daljeet and continued, 'No. As per court rules, that is not allowed.'

'The absence of a child in a four year – long marriage is a big question, your honour. It is hard to believe that Daljeet wouldn't have undergone a fertility test till date,' I said.

'It is clear Daljeet. You must be aware of your condition but always blamed Naina for your barren marriage. It is also possible that you might have known it before your marriage but didn't disclose it while getting married,' the judge said.

'No Sir, even I am shocked to know my condition,' Daljeet said, falling short of words to say anything further.

'Your submission, Advocate Kabir,' the judge said.

'Me lord, a marital knot loosens only if love between two people fades out. So what if a couple is childless? Love is something which has to prevail. A couple can remain happy even if they don't have a child,' Kabir threw his baseless argument.

'Let's keep the love-wave philosophy aside my lord, but here Daljeet and his family should have disclosed about his infertility to my client's family before marriage,' I intervened.

'Yeah... Daljeet must have got a dream before marriage that he had this issue!' Kabir said.

'If not before marriage, then at least after marriage! If a couple isn't blessed with a child, I guess the primary sperm count and sperm motility test should be conducted on males before going for more expensive and complicated fertility tests for women. Did Daljeet do that? No, your honour. He kept on blaming my client for that,' I said.

'Advocate Kabir, your client should have got himself diagnosed. He never did so and put everything on his wife. His fault is proven,' the judge said to Kabir.

'Me lord, I agree that my client didn't go for his sperm test. But the barrenness of their wedlock never brought any dents in their relationship. He and his family constantly strived to balance things out for Naina. But she was in her own trance. She wanted to live her life according to her own terms. Finally, things went overboard and Naina ran back to her parents,' Kabir threw a baseless argument again.

'Objection my lord, my client didn't run back to her parents. She... whatever... now I'd like to submit some documents to the court, with your permission,' I said.

'Go ahead.'

I took the 60–paged file of Blue Panther detective agency's confidential report prepared by Prakash Rajput and his team and gave it to the coordinator, who in turn passed it on to the judge. One-to-one murmurs ran across the courtroom with everyone wanting to know what the file was all about. I stole a glance at Daljeet – he wore a blank expression and kept looking at that file.

The judge ordered the attendees to be quiet and took a while to go through the file. He was shocked to read its contents but preferred not to disclose it in the courtroom. As the report was churned out of Blue Panther detective agency, it was taken seriously, for Prakash Rajput's confidential reports were known to be 100% accurate and admissible in the court. They had helped many a case to crack in the courts earlier.

'Advocate Kabir, this is the confidential report of your client Daljeet Singh Khurana. It speaks volumes about him,' the judge said.

'Pardon me your honour, but how much can we rely on this report? It may be a fabricated one. How can the court follow its contents?' a baffled Kabir asked.

'This is Prakash Rajput's report, Advocate Kabir. Every page has his agency's seal and a 3-D hologram. He has signed on all the pages as well. Blue Panther's report is an admissible evidence in court,' the judge said.

'I'd like to reiterate a few things on Daljeet Singh Khurana and his family, your honour,' I said.

'Permission granted.'

'As per the contents of this report, your honour, Daljeet Singh Khurana was married prior to his marriage with my client Naina,' I said.

The entire courtroom went berserk on hearing this. Daljeet and Kabir gave a perfect surprised expression to each other. Naina and her family were unable to meet anybody's eyes; they just kept gazing down.

'Your honour, I think my capable –' Kabir said as I interrupted him, 'Please let me complete, my lord.'

'Advocate Kabir, let him finish what he has to say,' the judge said.

'His ex-wife had committed suicide owing to excessive torture and dowry demands from Daljeet Singh Khurana and his family. But because nothing could be proven against him or any of his family members, Daljeet walked out free after a brief legal procedure. He couldn't have a child with his ex-wife too. He went for a fertility test then, and came to know that he was a sterile man,' I said.

All the court attendees were baffled to hear these facts about Daljeet. Had the legal reins been in my hands, I would have pushed Daljeet in a furnace then and there itself.

'Furthermore, Daljeet Singh Khurana had his own motor

garage in Sion Koliwada area once. His ex in-laws had even given him around three lakhs to upgrade it, but to no avail. All the money was spent in boozing and making merry. Now he wants to start his own car servicing showroom and demands twelve lakhs from my client's parents. In all this, he couldn't withstand constant refusals from my client. So that night he and his brother Harlot Singh Khurana raped her and threw her to glory hospital after which they never came to take her. That's all, your honour,' I said. I preferred not to make the mention of my key eye witness, Hariram at that moment as per our strategy.

'Mrs. Naina Daljeet Khurana, did you or your parents, friends or relatives conduct a background check on Daljeet Singh Khurana and his family before marriage?' the judge asked Naina.

'No Sir,' Naina said, gazing on the floor.

Turning towards Daljeet, the judge continued, 'Mr. Daljeet Singh Khurana, your confidential report alleges a lot against you for your past and present. Do you have anything to say in this?'

'Excuse me, your honour,' Kabir stepped in, 'We have been discussing that my client Daljeet and his brother Harjot raped Naina and all that… but can this be proven in this court? Did anyone see this?' Kabir said.

'This could have been medically proven, had they not used a protection that night. And thanks to those corrupt police officials who took cash and closed the case,' Naina interceded.

'Mrs. Naina, please do not interrupt again,' the judge said.

'There's an eye-witness to this incident, your honour,' I said as I gave a frowned look at Daljeet.

The moment I uttered these *most awaited* words, Daljeet looked at Harjot with a who-could-he-be expression. All the people sitting in the courtroom started discussing this case with each other as if they were lawyers and judges themselves! A collective wave of surprise, shock and optimism ran through Naina, her family, Aarti and Payal. Kabir dramatically threw his hands up in air and said, 'Now that's a new twist in this case, your honour! Where on earth has the so-called eye-witness come from? Where was he till date?'

'This is the advanced notice to the court and my opponent lawyer to produce the eye-witness in the next hearing,' I said as I handed the advance notice papers to the coordinator, who passed it on to the judge.

'Alright. You may produce the eye-witness to this case in the next hearing. It will be on the eighteenth of May. We break for lunch now,' the judge announced as he read my notice.

16

Third hearing of Naina Khurana v/s Daljeet Khurana case.

Mumbai High Court,
Dr. Kane Road, Fort, Mumbai.

Judge – Hon. Justice Sohrabjee Billimoria.

The third hearing of Naina's case witnessed twice the number of attendees in the court. Reporters from *Mumbai Mirror, Mid - Day, DNA* and *Dainik Jagran* marked their presence. The courtroom was overcrowded, so much so that the constabulary had to prevent further people from entering. Under instructions to the police from the High Court, additional force had been deployed in and out of the courtroom to control the mob, just in case it went frenzy on Daljeet and Harjot. Representatives of three prominent NGOs which worked for the emancipation of widows and the affected womenfolk were also present in the court. It was later learnt that they had already given a statement to media that if the court didn't give justice to Naina, they would take her under their wings.

'Advocate Aakash Khanna, before you produce the eye-witness for Naina Daljeet Khurana rape case, please continue with the case and strengthen it,' Justice Sohrabjee Billimoria said as the third hearing of Naina's case began.

'Thank you, my lord,' I said as I refreshed the case details to the court, 'My client Naina Daljeet Khurana, wife of Daljeet Singh Khurana, has accused her husband of physical harassment, incessant dowry demands and marital rape. Not only Daljeet Singh Khurana, his younger brother Harjot Singh Khurana is also accused of raping her. I have already submitted the background reference report of the Khuranas to the court in the previous hearing which proves many things against them, especially Daljeet Singh Khurana.'

'Your witness, please,' the judge turned to Kabir and said.

'Your honour, as we all know, Naina Daljeet Khurana accuses her husband and his brother of raping her. But medically it isn't proven – no semen traces were found inside her. Doctors confirmed it merely by looking at her condition and going by her statements. In addition to all this, we shouldn't brush the fact aside that the Khuranas live as a joint family. So how is it possible that a woman gets raped by two drunken men and nobody hears her screams and comes for help?' Kabir said. As per our plan, he was to make an indirect mention of the eye-witness by himself.

'I'll come to it in a few more moments, me lord. Nevertheless, a detailed analysis of the background reference report of Daljeet Singh Khurana states that he and his family are extremely money – minded people. Their sole intention in getting Daljeet married to my client was to extract money from my client's parents. They even did so, till their budget allowed them. But it couldn't douse the craving of Daljeet Singh Khurana and his family. All the call records, character report of Daljeet, statements of persons involved… everything is mentioned in the report. Let's leave everything aside your honour, I just have a simple question for Daljeet – why did he and his family hide his first marriage details to Naina and her family while getting married to her?' I said. This was precisely as per our plan – Kabir had to compel the judge to demand at least one eye-witness for the incident and I had to simultaneously lay a trap for the Khuranas.

Acute silence filled the courtroom. Press reporters were busy making the excerpts of the hearing. Court stenographers recorded all the statements, arguments and facts presented therein.

'Sometimes we have to forget our past and start our life afresh. It is not necessary to dig every small thing out and mention it to everyone,' Kabir threw an unsubstantiated statement.

'The court does not agree with your argument, Advocate Kabir. It was mandatory for Daljeet Singh Khurana and his family to disclose the fact that he was married earlier. But they didn't. The court will deal with the sentence for this at the end of this case. Nonetheless, Advocate Aakash, now please present the eye-witness in the court,' the judge said.

Kabir didn't say anything further. His job was to weaken the case gradually from his end and he was doing it amazingly.

I summoned one of the constables to bring Hariram in the courtroom. I and Kabir had decided to keep him out of the courtroom till the day and time his actual presence wasn't needed. The constable went out and brought Hariram in a few moments. As the courtroom was overcrowded, neither Daljeet nor Harjot could see him till he came to the witness box.

I asked Hariram to go to the witness box. The moment Daljeet and Harjot saw him, they got infuriated. But before they could bawl out on him, I said, 'Your honour, my opponent Daljeet Singh Khurana and his brother Harjot Singh Khurana may be told to maintain the decorum of this court, which I guess, they are going to spoil any moment.'

'Advocate Kabir, please instruct your client not to speak in between the eye-witness's oral submission,' the judge said to Kabir.

'Sure, my lord,' Kabir said as he signaled Daljeet and Harjot to keep calm.

'Your honour, he is the prime witness to my client, Naina Daljeet Khurana's rape incident of that night. Not only does Blue Panther detective agency's report testify him, even I have personally spoken to him and gathered all the facts. He witnessed that night's incident in parts. He shall give the court all the details of that night and what happened after that,' I said.

'What's your name?' the judge asked Hariram.

'I am Hariram Patangrao Naik, *sahab*,' Hariram said as he folded his hands and bowed to the judge.

'Since when have you been working at Daljeet Singh Khurana's place?' the judge asked.

'I worked for them for nearly eight years, *sahab*. But now I'm back to my home town, Nashik. Now I stay with my family and work there itself,' Hariram said.

'Why did you leave your job at Daljeet Singh's place?'

'I didn't leave *sahab*. They asked me to go back.'

'Did they give you any particular reason?'

'No *sahab*.'

'Hariram, did you see what happened with Naina that

night?' the judge came to the point.

'Yes, *sahab*. It must be around one thirty or two at night. I heard some screams from Naina *didi's* room. I heard her screaming enough is enough… what are you doing… leave me… and so on. I went and knocked the door of her room. To my surprise, Harjot *bhaiya* opened the door and told that Naina *didi* had a stomach ache. He smelt of alcohol as he spoke. I even asked him if *didi* needed anything, but he just refused and shut the door on my face,' Hariram narrated the ordeal of that night.

'Then?' the judge prodded as the stenographers recorded Hariram's statement on their PCs. Everybody listened to him with rapt attention.

'I went back to the kitchen where I used to sleep every night. But I couldn't sleep *sahab*. I could hear Naina *didi's* screams intermittently. Harjot *bhaiya* smelling of alcohol and opening the door of Naina *didi's* room disturbed my mind. He even told that she didn't need anything, whereas he himself told me that she had a stomach ache. I lay on the floor with my gaze fixed on Naina *didi's* room. After some time, they opened the door. They means Harjot *bhaiya* and Daljeet *bhaiya*. I saw them dragging Naina *didi* towards the entrance door. They didn't realize that I was watching them. In no time, they started the car and took Naina *didi* somewhere,' Hariram said.

'But why did they ask you to leave your eight year old service? Weren't they happy with you?' the judge asked Hariram.

'No *sahab*, there was no fault in me or my services. That's the reason I could do my job in their house for nearly eight long years. But Daljeet *bhaiya* called me the very next day and all of a sudden asked me to leave. I asked him to give me at least one reason to fire me, but all what he told was that, they no longer needed me. So that's how they threw me out, much like a fly out of a glass of milk. I went back to my home town at Nashik, and since then I have been staying with my family. I now work for a local wine shop as their godown supervisor *sahab*,' Hariram said.

'Advocate Kabir, would you like to cross examine the witness?' the judge asked.

'No, my lord,' Kabir replied as per our plan.

'So that's the whole story, your honour,' I said, 'The Khurana brothers have not only committed a heinous crime, but have also hidden the facts and attempted to keep the witness as far as possible from this case, which clearly indicates that they have committed the crime in question. My lord, now I would like to call Harjot Singh Khurana in the witness box.'

'Permission granted.'

The court peon called for Harjot to come in the witness box. He followed suit.

'Harjot Singh Khurana, you just heard what your ex-servant Hariram told to the court. Do you agree to all that?' I asked him.

Harjot didn't answer. He just kept looking at the floor.

'I repeat Harjot Singh Khurana, do you agree with whatever your ex-servant Hariram told to the court?' I said.

'Yes,' Harjot replied in as low a tone as possible.

'No further questions, my lord. Harjot, you can go back,' I said.

'So that's the whole story, your honour. Daljeet Singh Khurana and his brother not only raped Naina that night, but also dumped her in glory hospital and went away. I have the CCTV grabs of their entering and exiting the hospital, and also the writ statements of the hospital staff, most importantly of Dr Sulbha Sareen who had attended Naina that night. If need be, I can even produce them in the court. That's all, my lord,' I said.

'Advocate Kabir, would you like to say anything in this?' the judge asked Kabir.

'No, your honour,' Kabir said, going by our plan. By now, we had successfully tilted the scale almost in Naina's favour.

'The court has heard the statements of both the lawyers. Statement of the prime eye-witness, Hariram is also recorded and taken into consideration. The date of the fourth hearing of this case is twenty fifth of May. This court is adjourned for the day,' the judge announced.

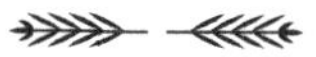

17

Fourth hearing of Naina Khurana v/s Daljeet Khurana case.

Mumbai High Court,
Dr. Kane Road, Fort, Mumbai.

Judge – Hon. Justice Sohrabjee Billimoria.

Mumbai High Court had never witnessed such a chaos in the recent times. People flocked in the courtyard by hundreds, with everyone of them sympathizing with Naina. A large group of women was seen holding boards and banners with slogans like *JUSTICE FOR NAINA, NAINA IS INNOCENT, PUNISH KHURANA BROTHERS, HANG DALJEET* and *NAINA – WE ARE WITH YOU.* It was a tough time for Mumbai Police to control the mob. Additional force from Thane Police had to be deployed in case of public outcry.

The moment Daljeet and Harjot stepped out of the police van, people started shouting slogans against them. One irate fellow even threw his sandal which hit right on Harjot's face, though the duo was gheraod by four police inspectors, four head constables and three constables and taken inside the courtroom. A little while later Naina arrived with her family. The moment she stepped out of her car, all the people present over there began shouting, 'NAINA – WE ARE WITH YOU.' Naina received an overwhelming support from the people of Mumbai. One of the women from the mob somehow managed to come to Naina and shouted at her, 'I will burn this court today if you do not get justice Naina.' Six lady constables formed a human barricade and escorted Naina and her family till the courtroom. All this was captured by the reporters and photojournalists of prominent news channels like Aaj Tak, Star News and Zee News, and aired on their respective channels. Live!

The courtroom was filled to the brim with the attendees.

People were struggling for every square inch of space to even stand inside. Soon, the proceedings commenced as Justice Sohrabjee Billimoria took his seat and announced, 'This court has listened to both the parties and their respective lawyers in the preceding hearings. Now I instruct the lawyers to conclude their arguments. Advocate Aakash, you may begin.'

'Thank you, my lord,' I said as I got up, 'My client, Naina Daljeet Khurana got married to Daljeet Singh Khurana around four years back. She did all what was expected out of her, almost blindfolded. Over a period of those four years, she has undergone tremendous mental harassment and even physical torture. Every woman yearns for a child after marriage, my lord. Every married woman wants to be a mother. So did Naina. She kept on telling her husband about this, but all what she got in return was slaps, abuses and forced sex. Still she tolerated everything but did not leak out a single thing to her parents who had instilled good virtues in her right from the beginning. She could have opted to walk out of her marriage long back, but she didn't. She understood the value of a marital knot and preserved it as nicely as she could. But things took a violent turn when her husband Daljeet Singh Khurana and his brother Harjot Singh Khurana raped her in an inebriated state and dumped her in the hospital. Subsequent investigation threw light on many facts. Firstly, Daljeet was married prior to getting married to my client Naina. His ex-wife had committed suicide as she couldn't withstand the torture inflicted by Daljeet. Secondly, Daljeet kept on elbowing my client to bring a hefty sum of twelve lakh rupees from her father. Is this why he took the seven marriage vows with her? Look at her condition, your honour. There's no charm left in her life now. How will she live the rest of her life? She is a household name today. Everyone is talking about her; everyone wants to sympathize with her. But let me tell you one thing, my lord – my client does not need anybody's sympathy. All what she wants is a severe punishment for the one who played around with her life instead of safeguarding it – Daljeet Singh Khurana. And as far as Harjot Singh Khurana is concerned, well, I insist the court to first cut both his wrists and separate them from his body before hanging him. Naina had been tying a *rakhee* on his wrist all these years. And in turn, instead of protecting her as his sister, he raped her! I have already submitted the background reference report of both of them and also the written statements of the hospital staff where Naina was being admitted. Most importantly, I have produced the eye-witness, Hariram Naik who saw Daljeet and Harjot drag Naina out of the house on that fateful night. So in view of my abovesaid statements and the facts presented, I request the court to charge the Khurana brothers with at least twenty years of rigorous imprisonment. That's all, my lord.'

All the attendees gave a standing ovation to me as I concluded my argument. The entire courtroom echoed with the sounds of claps and whistles which lasted for almost twenty seconds.

'Order, order! Silence please,' the judge attempted to silence the much – excited crowd. After several attempts, he could manage it.

'Advocate Kabir, please conclude your argument,' the judge said as he turned to Kabir. This was the final opportunity for him to weaken the case as much as he could, without seeming obvious.

'Thank you, your honour,' Kabir said as he got up, 'It is always seen that if the litigant or even the petitioner is a lady, people automatically offer her their sympathy absolutely free of cost! I can see the same thing happening here. Nobody is concerned about the future of my clients. Just because they are males, everybody, and I guess even the court thinks that they are at fault. But let me also tell you one thing, your honour – things can be manipulated. People can be bought. Situations can be altered if one uses his brain, power, money or all at a time. Why can't it happen that my capable opponent lawyer must have bribed the detective agency and made a false report of my client? After all, it is just a report, right? Is it a written rule that whatever be written in that confidential report ought to be true and followed in a court of law? I challenge the contents of this report, my lord. I claim that the facts contained therein are false or at least not hundred percent true. As far as my client's first marriage is concerned, well, my client and his family had clearly disclosed it to Naina Khurana and her family while getting married. But they turned hostile from the very first hearing itself. Secondly, how can the court rule out the possibility of the only eye-witness, Hariram being bribed to give a false statement which falls in Naina Khurana's favour? It is quite possible, your honour. Dignity rests not only with Naina Daljeet Khurana, but also with my client. So in my above views, possibilities and citations, I request the court to let my clients, Daljeet Singh Khurana and Harjot Singh Khurana walk free without any charges. I also urge the court to instruct my opponent, Naina Daljeet Khurana to pay a compensation of twenty lakhs to my client for her attempt to defame him and his family. That's all your honour.'

A collective wave of one-to-one murmurs ran across the court. It was quiet obvious that nobody agreed with the statements of Kabir who could successfully manage the stupidity in his concluding argument, as per our plan.

Justice Sohrabjee Billimoria did a final scrutiny of the statement files and case papers before giving his judgment. All eyes were glued to him. I stole a glance at Naina. To my surprise, she was looking at me with some hope in her eyes. I could renounce my world for that hope in her. She looked at the judge the moment our eyes met.

'This court has listened to the statements and arguments of both the litigants. Facts mentioned in the confidential report of Blue Panther detective agency, statements of the staff of glory hospital, CCTV footage of glory hospital and statement of the eye witness, Hariram Patangrao Naik are taken into consideration by the court,' the judge said as he paused for a moment and adjusted his spectacles.

'It is not uncommon these days to learn what a woman has to undergo if she goes in wrong hands after marriage. The basic problem lies with the ever increasing quantum of tolerance what today's women have. They keep on tolerating everything what keeps coming in their way, good or bad. And very few of them knock the doors of a court to attain justice. And courts keep prolonging their cases, demanding one document after the other. This has been happening in our country since ages. But it won't happen today.'

Justice Sohrabjee Billimoria's last sentence startled everyone present in the court. I crossed my fingers and prayed to God.

He continued, 'Naina's parents married their daughter to Daljeet without bothering to see his past record. Here, they did the right thing in a wrong way. After marriage, Naina endured all what she shouldn't have. There she did the wrong thing in a right way. And Daljeet gave her nothing but humiliation, pain and suffering all through their married life. Here he did the wrong thing in a wrong way.'

All the attendees collectively agreed with him with a *hmm*-sound which whizzed through the court. Press reporters and court stenographers wrote as fast as they could. Finally the most – awaited moment arrived when the judge announced his verdict.

'So, in Naina Daljeet Khurana rape case, vide chargesheet number 42313, taking into account the arguments submitted by Advocate Aakash Khanna, evidences against Daljeet Singh Khurana and Harjot Singh Khurana with reference to their confidential report by Blue Panther detective agency, statement of their servant Hariram and subsequent confession made by Harjot Singh Khurana, this court finds Daljeet Singh Khurana and his brother Harjot Singh Khurana guilty under sections 498A, 307, 376 and 34 of the Indian Penal Code and sentences them to a rigourous imprisonment for twenty years. It may be further noted that Naina Daljeet Khurana be granted a divorce immediately from Daljeet Singh Khurana without any further altercations and hearings for the same. This court is adjourned for the day.'

The moment Justice Sohrabjee Billimoria announced his verdict, all the attendees screamed in happiness and gave a standing ovation to him for nearly a minute. Everybody cheered and whistled as the joy in the hearts of Naina's parents knew no bounds. Naina wept incessantly as Nisha hugged her as tightly as she could. Soon, senior police constables hurriedly rushed to the witness box, handcuffed Daljeet and Harjot by their wrists and escorted them to judicial custody.

I gave a thumbs up to Naina and her parents. Her father came to me with folded hands and said, 'Aakash *beta*, I have no words to thank you. You have saved my daughter's life. You and Kabir have mended the biggest mistake what I did in my life.'

'That's my job, uncle,' I said as I smiled and held his hands.

'Convey our thanks to Kabir too. Tell him that I shall call him tomorrow,' Naina's father said and went back to Naina.

As the attendees left the courtroom, I collected my files and belongings when Naina came to me with Nisha. 'Aakash... thank you!' she said. A freshly wept Naina looked all the more gorgeous to me!

'That's alright Naina. You deserve justice. He deserves punishment. Now he won't see a rising sun for the next two decades, be rest assured,' I said as I winked.

'Thanks again Aakash,' Naina said as she went back to her parents.

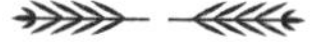

18

'I don't believe that! Man, what a perfect game plan you guys worked out!' Karan exclaimed as Aakash finished narrating his story. It was 10:30 PM. Patrons of Charmaigne Bar & Restaurant slowly began to leave.

'I've never seen opponent lawyers work like this. Aakash, Kabir, congratulations! Well done! Very well done! I'm proud of you guys,' Karan continued.

'Thanks Karan,' Kabir said as he slouched on his chair, 'But there are several questions here. Why did things go so awry that Naina had to knock the doors of a court? Two, why did Daljeet live his life the way he did? Three, why did I and Aakash devise a game plan to free Naina?'

Karan went silent. He had no answer to Kabir's questions, or perhaps he was too soaked up in Naina's story to answer either of them.

'That's a never ending debate guys,' Aakash stepped in as he signaled the waiter for the bill.

One week later…

Aakash was about to leave for his office as his phone buzzed of an SMS from Naina. She wrote –
Hi aakash! cn u cum over 2 payalz plac dis eve?
He replied –
Al well?
She wrote –
Ys. Need 2 tlk 2 u. hv cld kabir also.
He replied –
K. 6 pm wl b fyn??
She wrote –
K.

Aakash immediately called up Kabir and asked him, 'Has Naina called you too at Payal's place this evening?'

'Yes, she has. I guess she has called you also,' Kabir replied.

'Hmm. But why has she called both of us? Did Daljeet's family move to Supreme Court or what?' Aakash wondered.

'Balls to that Daljeet, man! Listen… pick me at five thirty from my office. I had a flat tyre last night. My car is towed by the mechanic,' Kabir said.

'Sure!'

***

Aakash pressed the doorbell of Payal's flat at 6:10 PM sharp. It was on the fourteenth floor of Raja Heights, an eighteen – storied tower at Mumbai Central.

'Yes?' the maid said as she opened the door.

'We have come to meet Payal,' Kabir said. The maid asked us to wait outside. In a few moments, Payal came to the door to receive us.

'Hi guys! Come come come…'

'Hi Payal!' Aakash and Kabir greeted her in unison as they entered. She asked them to follow her to her room. Boy, it was a lavish four – bedroom hall apartment overlooking the Arabian Sea!

As they entered her room, they saw Naina sitting by the window. She was lost in deep thoughts; Aakash could gauge it in a jiffy.

'Hi Naina!' Aakash greeted her. It disrupted her chain of thoughts.

'Hi Aakash! Hi Kabir!' she said. Kabir gave her a pleasant smile.

Summoning her maid for coffee and muffins for everyone, Payal came to the point. 'Guys, Naina wanted to say something to both of you.'

'Any problem from Daljeet's family?' Aakash instantly asked. Kabir gave him a frowned look.

'No no, nothing of that sort. Naina…' Payal said as she signaled Naina to speak further.

'Aakash, Kabir, I wanted to thank both of you from the

bottom of my heart. Had it not been for your strategy in the court, I would not be having a liberated life today. I feel so unburdened,' Naina said as a drop of tear rolled down her cheek.

'Don't be silly Naina. We all are friends and will always be there in each other's thicks and thins. And we haven't done anything extraordinary in your case. A little investigation here and there, four hearings in the court and lo! We got what we wanted. So chill,' Kabir said in an attempt to relax her. Aakash mentally admired him.

'That's very modest of you Kabir,' Naina said as the maid arrived with a large tray containing a pot of coffee, four mugs and a plate of tutty frutti muffins. She kept the tray on the table and went. Payal filled all the mugs with brewing hot, extra strong coffee and passed a mug to each of them.

'What happened Naina?' Aakash asked her, 'I guess you wanted to ask or inform us something…'

'What are your fees, guys? I need to make the payment,' Naina came to the point as she took the first sip from her mug.

'You called us here to discuss the fee part?' Aakash asked her in a dazed tone.

'Yes. All along these days, you guys went on working and strategizing things. But now it's time for me to pay both of you. How much does that bill for?' Naina asked.

'Zero!' Aakash and Kabir replied in chorus. They had already decided not to charge anything from her.

'What? No ways! Please tell me guys, how much I have to pay you,' Naina prodded again.

'Nothing, Naina. We had already decided that we won't charge anything from you. You think we did all this to earn money? If you think so, you've mistaken Naina,' Aakash said as he took a bite of his muffin.

'Then why did you guys fight so much for me?' Naina asked.

'For the sake of justice, friendship and punishing the guilty. Period,' Kabir said.

'Try to understand Aakash, I *have to* pay your fees. Kabir, you too,' Naina almost pleaded.

'No Naina. We won't take anything. Relax now. Eat a muffin,' Kabir said as he passed on the plate of muffins to her.

One month later…

'Bro, I think I should reveal my feelings to Naina. I'm ready for a lifelong commitment,' Aakash said to Kabir. They were on their way to their regular Bar Council meetings.

'Aakash, may I ask you one thing?' Kabir said.

'Yeah sure.'

'Don't misunderstand me… but will your extended family accept her? I guess they know by now that she is a –' Kabir said as Aakash interrupted him.

'Divorcee? Rape victim? That's what you want to say, right?'

'I'm sorry, I just –' Kabir said as Aakash interrupted him again.

'No brother, don't be sorry. It was written in her destiny. But for me, she's still as pure as before,' he said.

'Does she feel the same for you?' Kabir asked.

'Yes. I am cent percent sure. Though, she won't take the first step. I'll initiate it soon,' Aakash said as they reached the Bar Council of Maharashtra and Goa at Mumbai High Court extension, Fort.

It was one of the biggest challenges for Aakash to propose Naina for marriage and make her say yes. Sending a rose bouquet to her place with a *Will You Marry Me?* card… Talking to Nisha to convince her sister… Directly approaching her parents with a marriage proposal… he came up with all the ideas – sensible and weird. Finally, something struck his mind. He decided to propose Naina in the same coffee shop where he did years ago.

***

'CCD? Why?' Naina asked Aakash. He called her from his office after calling it a day.

'I have something very important to tell you. It concerns my life. My future,' he said, rather hinted.

Naina got the hint. She went quiet.

'Hullo, you there?' Aakash said.

'Hmm,' Naina *hmm*-ed.

'So CCD. Tomorrow. Five in the evening. You'll come?' Aakash asked.

'OK', Naina said and hung up.

Next day, Aakash finished all his appointments and freed himself by four in the afternoon. He started for Café Coffee Day outlet of Dadar east at 4:30 PM sharp. En route, he bought an assorted bouquet of lilies, orchids and roses. He alighted from his cab and entered the café at 4:55 PM sharp.

The café was exactly the same as it was before. Circular glass tables… cushioned cane and wooden chairs… posters on the walls… it was as if his good old college times were back. For a few moments, Aakash stood still with the bouquet in his hand. Soon, a stewardess came to him and disrupted his oblivion, 'Table for one, Sir?'

'Eh? Oh… Yes. I mean… no, table for two,' Aakash fumbled. The very sight of the interiors of the café brought back memories of the day when he had proposed Naina and got rejected.

'I'll prefer to sit there,' Aakash said to the stewardess, pointing out to the same chair which he had taken the last time.

'Sure!' the stewardess said as she went to the counter.

Naina arrived at 5:15 PM. 'I'm sorry Aakash… Was stuck in traffic…'

Naina's words refreshed their memory. She was *stuck in traffic* last time too!

'Traffic? How would I know that there's traffic in Mumbai? I just came from Bihar this morning *na*…' Aakash said, rather, repeated what he had told her last time.

Naina didn't react. She took her seat opposite to Aakash. She stole a glance at the bouquet kept on the table but didn't ask about it.

'What will you have?' Aakash asked her after a brief silence of ten seconds.

'Coffee.'

'Fine,' Aakash said as he signaled the steward for two

coffees.

'Why have we come here Aakash?' Naina asked him. It's a well-known fact that girls ask a question despite knowing its exact reply. And Aakash knew that!

'Naina I want to tell you something. It's serious. I don't want to delay. And I don't want to beat around the bush either,' Aakash said in one breath.

Naina kept looking at him for a few moments. Her eyes had a million things to say. Finally she spoke, 'What is it Aakash?'

Aakash took a deep breath and began, 'Naina, when two people unite for the institution of marriage, there are certain strings attached to it – legal, logical and straight from the heart. All seems good in the initial phases; the real test of tolerance, endurance and most importantly, love begins later on. Being a girl from a middle-class family, you chose to go according to your parents' choice. You didn't even care to know the person with whom you were to spend your entire life. And that was your biggest mistake Naina.'

The steward came with two cups of steaming coffee. He kept the cups with sachets of brown and white powdered sugar on our table and went.

'To put it honestly, had it not been for Kabir's sincere cooperation, we would probably still be tangled in legal mess,' Aakash continued as he took the first sip of his coffee.

'I would always be indebted to you both, for your strategy helped me to undo my and my family's mistake,' Naina said.

Aakash smiled. 'We did all that only to give justice to you as we knew you weren't at fault Naina... that you were speaking the truth,' he said.

'Thanks Aakash. But why did you call me here?' Naina asked.

Aakash went on for a repeat performance, 'Past is past Naina. But looking at the future, I'd like to ask you one thing. Will you marry me?'

Naina kept looking at Aakash as she took a deep breath on hearing his proposal. Rather, a reproposal.

Aakash got up, took the bouquet in his hands and bent down on his knees. Then gathering all his might, he held Naina's hand and finally proposed, 'I love you Naina. I still love you. All these years I have loved you. I accept you the way you are. I want to marry you. Will you?'

Naina's eyes were filled with tears to the brim. Aakash kept looking at her. He waited for her reply.

'Aakash, it isn't that I didn't like you. And I'm sorry that I had to reject your proposal outright that day. We girls are not allowed to choose our life partners in my community. And I followed the same and landed where I am. But today I shall follow my heart,' Naina said.

Aakash asked her again, 'I want to marry you. I want to spent my entire life with you. I want to give you all what you desire and deserve Naina. You have always been an indispensible part of my life. Will you marry me?' and gave her the bouquet.

She accepted the bouquet and said, 'Yes. But first come and speak to my parents.'

Aakash's sincere feelings and the assortment of flowers did its job.

***

'She said yes!' Aakash said to Kabir. He called him after reaching home.

'Marvellous! What is the next step?' he asked.

'I need to go to her place and speak to her parents regarding this,' Aakash said.

'Sounds good. So when are you going?'

'This week itself. But hullo… you too are coming with me. I won't go alone,' Aakash said.

'Yup, I will. Why don't we go this Saturday? Say by evening…' Kabir suggested.

'Will do. I'll convey it to them. Thanks Kabir,' Aakash said and hung up.

***

Aakash made all possible attempts to look his best for

his Saturday rendezvous with the Gills. He brought himself an expensive shirt and a pair of trousers from the Park Avenue section of Shoppers Stop, Bandra. He instructed his receptionist to keep his last appointment at 4:00 PM on Saturday so that he could go back home, change into a prospective groom and proceed to meet Naina's family.

He picked Kabir from his office at 5:30 PM and the duo proceeded to Naina's place at Mahim. They reached there at 6:00 PM sharp.

'Welcome!' Nisha said as she opened the door. Naina's father folded back his newspaper as Aakash and Kabir entered the house. Reading newspapers happens to be a favourite time pass of retired people!

'Hello Aakash! Hello Kabir,' Naina's mother said as she briefly came out of the kitchen.

'Hello aunty!' Aakash and Kabir greeted her in unison.

'Please sit *beta*, I'm a bit busy in the kitchen. Make yourself comfortable,' she said.

'Sure! Thanks aunty,' Kabir said as Naina's mother went back to the kitchen.

'How are you uncle?' Aakash asked Naina's father.

'Good, *beta*. Retired... nothing much to do,' he said and smiled.

After a casual talk with the boys, Naina's father came to the point. 'Naina told us about your proposal, Aakash.'

'Yes uncle, she has told you the right thing. I want to marry her,' Aakash said to Naina's father, looking straight in his eyes.

There was a brief silence of five seconds. 'Call mom and Naina,' Naina's father said to Nisha. She went inside.

In a few moments, Naina came with a large tray in her hands containing savories enough to feed a small town. She was accompanied by her mother. Aakash was stunned to see her - she wore an Indian ethnic styled blue and pink coloured salwar suit with a matching dupatta. Her peacock feather-themed ear rings matched with her dress and complimented with her purple pendant. She looked gorgeous. Aakash fell in love with her for the second time.

Naina took her seat alongside her mother, diagonally opposite to Aakash who was seated bang opposite to her father. 'Please help yourself *beta*,' Naina's mother said to Aakash and Kabir.

'Sure aunty,' Aakash said as he and Kabir picked up a cup of tea each.

'Tell me Aakash...' Naina's father said to him.

Taking a sip of his ginger tea, Aakash went on to convince Naina's father for his daughter's hand. 'Uncle, I have always liked your Naina right from the days when we were studying law. Life took a violent turn for her after her marriage, and I'm really sorry for all the crap that happened with her. But she too deserves her own share of happiness, solace and contentment. Years ago, when I came to know about her marriage, I was heartbroken. But I could do nothing but give her best wishes for her married life,' Aakash said and paused to have the next sip of his tea. Everybody listened to him with grim attention.

'Years after that, when Naina came to me with her case, I laughed at our destinies. They were so intertwined... so much so that she came right to me, leaving hundreds of thousands of lawyers in Mumbai city! And that's when I realized that we indeed have a connection, a strong one. After her victory in the court, I decided to take things forward, for I still like her and want to spend my entire life with her. Yes Uncle – I love Naina. I want to marry her and give her all the things that she desires and is worthy of. Will you marry her off to me?' Aakash said. *Kudos to you, junior!* Kabir thought.

'*Beta*, that all is OK. But your parents didn't come...' Naina's mother asked Aakash.

'I lost my mother during my birth itself, aunty. Doctors could save either of us during my delivery. Dad told them to save mom. But due to some complications, they couldn't save her and instead saved me. My dad did everything single handedly and made me a lawyer. But he too passed away three years back due to a heart attack,' Aakash said.

'Sorry to know that,' Naina's mother said and passed a plate of samosas to Aakash and Kabir.

'Aakash, I only have one question for you,' Naina's father said, 'Will you keep our daughter happy?'

'Yes uncle. All along her journey, Naina has faced a lot. I promise to undo everything and give her a happy and content life,' Aakash said. Kabir smiled and nodded at Naina's parents.

'Naina, what's your say in this?' Naina's father asked her.

'As you say dad,' she replied.

***

Kabir handled all the preparations for Aakash's civil marriage with Naina. Aakash and Naina wanted to keep it simple. They applied at the marriage registrar of the Family Court, Bandra – Kurla Complex and submitted their relevant documents. After a month, they were called to sign on the legal marriage register with two witnesses each. Kabir and Karan witnessed from Aakash's end while Aarti and Payal did from Naina's end.

Aakash wanted to take Naina out for a few days after their marriage. As his wedding gift, Kabir gave them an entire honeymoon package for 7 days/ 8 nights of Jaipur, Jodhpur and Udaipur. Aarti and Payal collectively gifted the lovely couple a set of 18 carat gold plated Titan wrist watches. Naina's parents gifted a set of expensive gold rings to her and Aakash. Additionally, they even wanted to gift them two lakh rupees in cash, but it was politely declined by Aakash.

Everyone had come to the airport to see off the couple for their honeymoon. Aakash and Naina looked like the world's most blessed couple. Soon, the announcement for the Mumbai – Jaipur flight was made when Nisha came to Naina with teary eyes and said, 'Remember I told you *didi*… one day you'll get to live the life of your dreams.'

THE END